Soap Opera

Soap Opera

by
Mark R. Sneller

Published by Fresh Air Press

Visit Mark's website at
markrsneller.com

This edition was prepared for publication by
Ghost River Images
5350 East Fourth Street
Tucson, Arizona 85711
www.ghostriverimages.com

Cover images by permission
istockphotos.com

ISBN 978-1-7368917-6-6

Library of Congress Control Number: 2022910459

Printed in the United States of America
June, 2022

Other books Mark R. Sneller:

A Breath of Fresh Air

Greener Cleaner Indoor Air

Greener Cleaner Indoor Air – 2nd Edition

Toxic Exposure

Dying to Read

The Mars Virus Series

    The Mars Virus

    The City Beneath the Earth

    Treasures

Strange Adventures

Rising To Eminence

Prologue

In the early years of the Mars Virus, when it began to affect all plant and animal life, other events were occurring on a galactic scale. This was before the world turned upside down, before the tectonic plates shifted and Category 6 hurricanes ravaged the inland areas, before the polar ice caps melted and coastlines and islands disappeared and before volcanoes exploded around the world and billions died. In this story, comedy meets tragedy when humans meet aliens for the first time, all of whom question the meaning of their lives and recognize their common struggle for existence.

COVER-UP

FADE IN: INTERIOR OF FLYING SAU-
CER, CONTROL CABIN

"This is Anor Quinn broadcasting with the Galactic News Agency on site at planet Earth." He swept his three tentacles over his head and, with his middle arm, ensured they strung prop-erly down his neck taking it easy on the long one in the middle, the sensory tentacle, used for mating purposes.

Quinn continued, "Be advised: This is our season finale of our comedy series, *For the Love of Earth*. Today: Will the odd two-legged two-armed earthlings survive the arguments with their different linguistic, ethnic and political groups. Our experienced forecasters predict they will not. We'll listen in during the private conversations for some real hoots, so hang on to your vitals. Many of our paid subscribers ask the question: Who cares?"

It would be in their best interests to at least

hope that *something* occurred. As it stood, the less than popular series featuring earth's inhabitants had been slated for cancellation with sponsorship increasingly difficult to obtain. For general purposes, Anor did not want the planet to become a wasteland. But ratings were ratings. He was in the broadcast business, not the free-lucky-charms business.

FADE OUT FOR ADVERTISEMENTS BY THE SPONSORS: UNIVERSAL HEALTH FOODS, GALACTIC TOURIST LINES, DRESSES AND TRESSES FOR THE RICH AND FAMOUS, AND PERSONAL SECURITY BEFORE FAMILY

Now off the air, Anor declared to Jado, his identical twin brother, "These humans make me crazy. How the factions coexist is mind-boggling."

"That's just it, Anor, they don't, which makes for a successful comedy, especially when they actually try to coexist. Each faction will pick at the slightest thing to show its superiority," Jado declared with mirth.

Jado had been a mercenary for a couple of centuries. Tired of arms running and barely escaping death on a number of occasions, he finally decided to call it quits as a maker of news and contacted his brother for a legitimate job in reporting the news. Always bonded, but rarely in contact, Anor jumped at the chance for a partnership and recently got him a job with Galactic

News Agency, or GNA, as their first and only weapons specialist. Since then, the two joined to become a news team second to none.

The fact that a number of worlds listed Jado on their most wanted list did not concern anyone other than those who wanted him. Others lionized him as a freedom fighter. You couldn't ask for more press. The reborn Jado Quinn had become engaged in a new career; that of making an honest living. His word was his bond, which he gave GNA, up to a point.

They had parked their saucer on the dark side of earth's moon months before over intervals of several years. In between, they recorded more exciting events in the galaxy and always argued that a less valued reporting team could cover what they were ordered to do. Now, the time had arrived again to close out another season of boring broadcasts.

Their ship carried a dozen beings from various worlds, all of them expert in the fields of audio and visual photography, sound amplification, linguistics, intra-galactic navigation, nuclear physics, weaponry, and nuances pertaining thereto. The ship also contained the Quinn brothers, experts in theatrics and broadcasting.

GNA operated many such news vessels within the galaxy. The brothers' electronically-replete personal cabin contained a multi-species bathroom and a small bedroom with two bunk beds to house whomever might be present as guests. A score of screens were present around most of the saucer's interior, each featuring a different drama recorded from around the galaxy. Two exercise areas and a central galley provided enough food and supplies for every meal taste.

Beings from every world wanted to belong to the Quinn team. Only the best were approved and cared not where they might be stationed, as long as they were together as a unit. In the end, on paper, Anor made the final decisions.

Anor, all seven green feet of him, stood and stretched, waving his three arms about. He checked to ensure that his voice did not go out over the airwaves. "The earthlings just won't destroy each other and they keep teasing and teasing . . ."

"Anor, so don't get wrapped up in minutiae," declared Jado, and snapped a few of his digits. When the drinks arrived, Jado offered his brother a pair of medication tablets. Anor gratefully took them and swallowed. Soon, a door to the broadcast cabin of the spaceship opened and two attendants appeared carrying mind-altering substances in liquid form. Both Anor and Jado threw down the drinks in an instant. The attendants disappeared.

"I get that, Anor. I appreciate everything we have built and the money and position . . ." Jado sounded drunk as the alcohol and the medications began to take effect.

Inebriated or not, Jado did not exaggerate. Countless toys and do-dads were sold across the galaxy, each with images of himself and his brother to bring incredible wealth and fame to them both. He should be appreciative, Jado thought; although in all fairness, Anor had been popular well before he had stuck himself into the contract with GNA.

The brothers had a leaning toward eccentricity. Once off his medication, either could become unpredictable. Curiously, that contributed to their popularity. The audience loved a narrator with personality and flavor. During his younger years, Jado could remember when beings preferred warm and stable broadcasters, although none of them Semi-Transparents or Semi-Ts, of course. Anor changed all that to add enrichment to the stew.

Anor stood and lectured his brother, head-tendrils and body arms waving in all directions, manipulating keys on the console. The spacecraft drifted upwards to clear the edge of the moon to present them with a wondrous view of the planet in full sunlight. "A thousand years ago our people found this planetary dung heap and forecast that it would never amount to anything. So far they've been right. Virtually everything they've done has been predicted and it's been a hundred years since Network picked them up as a late night time slot—a cheap date, as it were. They're getting into space, so what?

I get that it's not prime time anymore, but, hey, we've done it all."

"Don't say 'so what'. We did lose a ship down there which may have aided their progress. It happened before you joined us," Anor said.

Jado held his brother around the shoulders and gently pushed him into the captain's chair. The seat instantly conformed to his shape to hold him securely and comfortably. "No argument from me. They're simpletons bent on self-annihilation and provide good entertainment for a large portion of our viewers."

FADE IN: OVERVIEW OF PLANET

Years before, miniature and undetectable video cameras had been shot into orbit from the GNA saucer and which surrounded the blue-green world. These saw and recorded anything the occupants of the ship wanted to record. Other cameras and recorders had been secreted in locations that might be handy on the planet itself, if called upon. Movement of persons and voices within buildings could be seen, heard and monitored. As a drama unfolded in one or more hot spots, the technicians would focus on that event around the clock, present Anor with the backdrop, and help him understand the unfolding events, thus better enabling him to narrate the occurrences that the galaxy-wide audience would watch.

Anor contemplated what they needed to do

next, now that this season's broadcasting had finished here. As per standard procedure, they'd need maybe a week or two of follow-up to clean up odds and ends. Their ship would leave the moon and would move faster than could be detected by any technology the people possessed. Even if they were detected upon their departure, what was one more saucer sighting?

The dictum of the politicians, who owned and ran GNA, held to a strict hand's-off policy and zero tolerance. Great broadcasters had been brought to ruin for even slight infractions. Well, too late now, Anor reflected. If things panned out, new events could certainly help next season's ratings and then do what . . . bring in more wealth? More fame? More glory? A dead world?

They risked losing everything if the present turn of events could be traced back to them. So far they had not needed to do anything here except for permitting the earthlings to see their spacecraft on occasion. Big deal. A tease to stir up the pot. That's not like creating a quake or assassinating a key figure or flooding an entire continent. They played the game within the rules, with one lone exception.

To swear they had never manipulated events would be a flat-out bald-faced lie. They had made the audience aware that a Pakistani general, in league with terrorists, had given the terrorists access to one of the nuclear vaults in Kandahar, the capital city of Pakistan, with a population of some 600,000. Fine unto itself. But in a drug-induced state, and not willing to let tens of millions of Americans die at the hands of terrorists, Anor wanted to explode a single bomb. This would result in the death of only a large portion of Kandahar.

If it could be proved that the explosion happened because of something they had done, their images would be hung in effigy, even in a universe full of beings tolerant of misdeeds. However, the galaxy's inhabitants would not be tolerant if they knew that Galactic News Agency had the means to bring about the death of one world, and as a logical sequitur, had the capability to bring out the death of their own. Therefore, the galactic federation had a strict hand-off policy.

As fate would have it, the photo shoot had concluded. Anor called the technical crew, congratulated them on a great job, told them to wrap up and prepare to go on home after they did their usual after season follow-up. They'd all meet at their usual pub in a couple or three weeks if another assignment didn't present itself. This was a real possibility because a love affair was ongoing between the King of Cartoom, Kredo Quinn, another of their brothers, and the Queen of Valencia, another triped, on their home planets a mere 500 light year apart. This affair promised to continue with hot and steamy episodes.

"That's our king," exclaimed Anor.

Jado nodded. "And our brother. It's no secret

he's sexually over-endowed. An issue of heredity," he confessed, pridefully. "In his case, he's in love with three arms, three legs, three breasts, three eyes, and three tentacles."

"There aren't a lot of Twos to chose from," Anor noted, then snorted in his fashion. "Look at bipeds. Heck, the slightest breeze and they blow over—no stability whatsoever. They even have to jump up to pick fruit when tentacles can do that. But don't mention that to a Semi-T.

"I have in front of me the results of a poll in which the vast percentage of viewers think the appearance of humans is, well, I don't want to use the word repulsive, so I won't. Let's just say that we should see if we could focus in more on natural disasters rather than showing the humans themselves. How they could even evolve with only two eyes and two ears is beyond me. How could they see what was sneaking up behind them? Even their four-legged creatures, from the smallest to the largest, have only two eyes and ears. And their fish. You have to get to their sixes and eights before multiple eyes show up!"

Ensuring the mike was still on, Anor continued, "Forget earth for a moment. Bragging aside, I know it's our brother and our home world, but maybe Kredo needs to clean up the rampant crime and corruption that's destroying Cartoom. He's too distracted."

Once Anor signed off with his crew, a chill

of fear overtook him and gave him a bad case of the shakes. "Let's finish what we have to do and get out of here."

Jado stared at his brother. "Look, things will take care of themselves. You know we may make things worse if we meddle."

"I'm thinking," responded Anor. "If we do explode a nuke, we could have a problem when GNA reviews the footage."

"Not if the crew isn't recording," responded Jado. "Look, I feel badly, too, If we did this, at least you and I will be the only ones who know the truth. We'll keep everyone else out of the loop."

The two shook six arms and sat down to compute a plan of action. Jado ticked off points on the ten digits of his middle and primary arm. "We know they brought in seven large trailers to haul off the bombs. We also know those trailers had been on stand-by since the new president came into office. That was back in episode four of the series before we switched to the typhoon off China. We followed the inspection of the nuclear storage facility by the United Nations and spied on the general when he called the terrorist leader to give him the eight digit code to open the electronic lock on the steel door to the concrete warehouse where the bombs were stored. Okay, so far?"

Anor agreed. "Indeed, if you recall, we dedicated the next episode to the volcanic eruption in Sumatra where 100,000 people tried to flee the pyroclastic cloud and either got asphyxiated or burned to death before being buried under 10 million tons of ash. Great episode. For some reason, though, the feedback we got was that the death and destruction were all right but there was no romance asssociated with it.

"After that, in the next episode, the big trucks, already on standby, load up with terrorists and move into the compound, kill the scant number of guards who are drinking and carousing with the local whores and not paying attention to their duties. The general has flown out of the country to a luxury villa in France, soon to be the world's most wanted man, while the terrorists enter the numbers given them to the vault, pick up five hydrogen and two neutron bombs with heavy forklifts and load them onto the vehicles. Our ratings skyrocket. End of story and end of the season."

Jado assented, "In for a finger, in for three arms. We trigger one of their nukes and blow up all the bad guys. "It'll look like they did it to themselves out of stupidity."

"Exactly." Anor's voice slit finally turned upward. "Now you're starting to use your brain."

"Here's the bad news," Jado expostulated. "The seven nuclear weapons have multiple safeguards. You can't set them off with explosives and you do have to set them off with a coded sequence and you have to know that code and you have to know how to arm them. The general gave them all they needed to know."

Anor thought for a moment, and lamented, "Okay, we know where those weapons are. Any school child can operate nuke sensors and pinpoint the location of radioactive weapons from outer space. But we don't have the codes to blow even one of them."

Jado clapped his brother on the shoulder. "Anor, here's a bit of good news. That technology is ancient. We can detonate one of the bombs with a pinpoint laser set at a thousand degrees and hit the junction past the timer and the input into the atom bomb that is used to trigger either the hydrogen or neutron bomb. Simple stuff. Been there, done that.

"So while you've been working and translating the story dialogue into Universal Galactic for the show, I've been on the job tracking the trucks. Bet you ten-to-one the cult leaders are nearby, certainly within the radius of a nuclear blast."

Jado pulled up a screen that depicted seven very slow moving trucks, each covered with a tarp. His imaging system penetrated the tarps to reveal the different weapons. The last two were the neutron bombs.

There was a lot Jado had not told him about his years as a merc, but when he signed on with GNA, he'd insisted that, if they were going to permit him to fly with his brother, their largest of all saucers must be outfitted with the latest in weaponry, second only to a battle cruiser. He rightly argued that a number of the GNA ships had come under attack by pirates in open space (including some by himself) and insisted on better protection. He presented his list of equipment he desired and insisted that GNA protect them. Tired of losing ships, HQ relented.

"If we blow one, won't they all go?" Anor asked.

"No, you can't trigger a nuclear bomb to go off with another nuclear blast, not even with these old relics. In any case, we want to blow up one of the neutron bombs. That will still kill people, but will leave structures intact. We don't need a radioactive cloud blowing into a large foreign population center.

"One more thing. We're going to have to hurry up because the military should be around pretty soon and the force from the blast will shut down the electronics of their vehicles and their planes. Remember, those are the good guys."

"That could mean the end of our show here," Anor said, smiling again, looking forward to working more quality programs and wishing he could have another dose of medication.

Jado commiserated. "Maybe. Don't forget there is no lack of terrorists on this planet. And, dear brother, if it is the end of the assignment, so what? The show is as much about us as it is about subject matter."

Jado operated the controls and shut down all the screens on the ship, standard procedure after a shoot, except for one in their private room. At the weapons console, he punched a button. A cross-hair appeared hovering over the trucks. He adjusted the crosshair, sharpened and minimized its image, moved it to the last bomb in the chain, enhanced the image, and depressed a red button. A bright light filled the screen.

"That's it?" inquired Anor.

"One and done," answered Jado.

"Now what?"asked Anor. "Stay here a few days and make sure everything is clean?"

Jado scratched his right armpit with his left arm and said, "All we have to figure out now, before we send in the footage, is how to explain what the stupid terrorists could have possibly done to a bomb in transit to make it blow up on its own."

Anor groaned.

Just at that moment the incoming call button flashed from GNA Central. The brothers gasped in unison wondering how their employer could have found out about what they had done in such short order. Rumor had it they had psychics on their staff.

Shakily, Anor pressed the receive button. "Anor here."

A voice on the other end spoke, "You guys about ready to finish out there?"

"We're just preparing for follow-up, sir."

"Send in what you've got and get over to Valencia. War may break out if King Goldura of finds out that his queen is making babies with the king of Cartoom. Not only that, but you've got the only warship in the fleet. We need you there *now*."

"Yes, sir, we're on our way. Quinn out."

Anor turned back to the screen and remarked, "If any crew member saw that explosion, he'd get suspicious."

Jado responded with a sly smile, "It'll be perfect. We'll put it on GNA."

"What? How so?"

"GNA will be between a rock and a hard place, as they say in English earth language. They ordered us to leave. Fine. The explosion will be a perfect wrap to the season—keep the viewers itching for the next series to begin. We'll title it, *Will Earth Survive?*"

They couldn't get away fast enough. While Jado got on the intercom and informed the crew of their new orders, Anor programmed the ship for the flight to Valencia to cover the developing story. Perhaps they would have a chance to get back home to Cartoom. At least they wouldn't have to travel to GNA Central on Butrys at the farther part of the galaxy, some 30,000 light years from where they were presently stationed.

If and when they returned to begin the following season, what were they to surmise if they came upon a dead world? Would it be that Pakistan had assumed that India had nuked them and returned the favor. Perhaps missiles had flown back and forth until an errant one hit on the outskirts of Tehran. This brought the Iranians into the act which brought in Israel, then Russia and the Americans and so forth until ten thousand missiles flew from silos and submarines.

The developing civilization, such as it was, might never have had a chance to achieve serious space flight. It might have been set-back a thousand centuries or more. On the good side, if that happened, perhaps GNA would be thankful that the series on earth could now be eliminated. The Quinns would be even more thankful, if GNA *never* found out what they had done. The job can be stressful at times.

QUEEN'S GAMBIT

Anor and Jado Quinn, along with their crew, managed to grab a few hours of food and rest while the crew landed the vessel out of sight on a moon to observe the seventh planet, dubbed Valencia.

Once they settled in, the crew chief contacted Jado in the control console. "Sir, we've got the palace locked on. They must know we're here because they're sending ships to greet us."

Anor replied, "No problem. We've got distance rights. Zero in on the castle and see what the queen is up to."

Jado inserted, "Under no circumstances do I want the welcoming party to believe we are anything but a news ship until I give the okay."

Almost instantly, a close-up of the castle appeared on one of the monitors. The queen's chamber appeared in another. Audio came on instantly. The military of the planet might see the GNA ship, but apparently the queen didn't. Not a fan of video dramas, her interests leaned toward the latest wearing apparel. She left the governing up to the king, which was all too infrequent.

In the presence of her handmaid, the queen succumbed to her ministrations. Her skin gleamed with bug oil, her three breasts shone in the light of the fluorescent lamps, her three loosely jointed arms waved about. The eye on either side of the forehead gleamed with excitement and expectation, while the eye on the back of her head was closed for the moment.

"Your husband has been gone for a long time my queen. So far there has been no word from him regarding your last baby. I shudder to think about what he would do were he to find out," offered the handmaid, expectantly awaiting to hear more intimate details.

The queen shrugged and gave a slight laugh. "I will make many more before his return. They will all remain with my sister," running her hands over her body sensually, in apparent expectation of her meeting with her lover, concerned that her babies were muntants, smarter, faster, and strongeer than any in past generations.

The film crew captured the scene, which would soon be transmitted to the tens of billions of sentient galactic beings, after video clean-up by production and GNA Central. Normally, this took a matter of seconds—minutes at the most. "My special king is on his way to feel the silky smoothness of my skin, the ripeness of my sexual organs; how he lusts for them. Soon he will have it all and then some."

"Rumor has it he may be amassing his forces to capture you, your highness, away from your king," contributed the maid, teasingly, hoping to go along for the ride, if it should ever happen, perhaps even to be captured herself.

The queen gave a smile as smooth as the rest of her body, "Oh, yes, it is so exciting that my pulse quickens and my juices flow." She shuttered to such an extent that the watching camera crew breathed harder.

"This beats terrorist scum on earth" said Anor, his sensory tentacle swelling with delight, as he spoke Jado's ear.

"Shut up, I want to listen," whispered Jado, lightly fingering his own sensory tentacle.

A tiny dot caught a ship leaving Cartoom. Another film crew already in orbit at the planet zoomed in on the tail markings and identified the ship as the private yacht of King Kredo Quinn, just before it entered the nether-realm of subspace.

The scene switched back to Valencia, where the queen's private phone rang. She picked it up, read something and smiled. Her prince in shining armor would soon be here.

In a bold move, six space ships, heavily loaded with armament, appeared from the backside of the planet. They weren't the GNA saucer types, but actual spaceships and were not a welcoming party. "Do they belong to the Valencian fleet?" asked Anor, broadcasting to the masses. "Do you think they're going to attack Kredo when his yacht appears?"

"No, there is no subterfuge here at the present time, according to my sources. I can only think the ships are going to guarantee him safe passage," replied Jado.

"I will admit he's a handsome devil. Voted by women as the best looking three-eyed three-legged three-tentacled being on Cartoom, or any other planet of threes, for that matter," Anor stated flatly.

Jado said, "Wait a second, give me a close shot of that lead ship," Jado called in the intercom to the crew, as he peered more closely into the tri-dimensional screen.

The film crew focused in on the lead ship only 100,000 thousand miles away in open space. "I know that vessel," said Jado quietly, almost to himself, "and I know the captain. It's Tantor the Tauntor. He's done jail time. He's totally demented. He must not know we're here. The creature hates GNA because we got him busted by filming his criminal acts. If he sees us, our mission could be in trouble. No, those aren't part of the Valencian navy; they're pirates and I'll bet you ten-to-one they're going to try to kidnap Kredo when he comes out of subspace. Anything in open space is fair game for this bunch, but they're not in open space, which makes them criminals."

Jado scanned the surrounding atmosphere near the ships and declared, not only to his brother and the crew, but to the viewing soap opera followers, "Notice you don't see any military craft after those ships. They must have paid off the military captain because we had no indication of a battle between the two groups. They won't hesitate to nuke a city to get what they want."

FADE OUT: COMMERCIAL MESSAGES FROM ALLSTAR TRAVEL, FLEX CLOTHING FOR ALL SHAPES AND SIZES, AND PUPU'S PLEASURE PLANET

FADE IN

The handmaid assisted the queen in putting on her garments. "You'll meet him here, then?" she asked. The camera crew had already discovered the spy hole used by the prurient handmaid when the queen had previously received her esteemed guest for their salacious encounters.

The queen checked herself in the mirror and unbuttoned the top button of the cloak that covered her breasts, thought for a moment, then unbuttoned the second one. She ran her hands over her stomach. "Yes, and it will be another baby tonight with my love." She spoke the intra-galactic language of the masses.

"Fortunately, your King Goldura will be gone for several more months," contributed the handmaid, already dripping sweat in anticipation of what she could see and capture from her spyhole camera to review at leisure.

"And that means several more babies," sighed Queen Tania, turning about in the mirror a number times. She placed a long tress of real synthetic hair over her head in the fashion of the rich and famous, leaving room for the foot-long tentacles to move about freely. The handmaid began to breathe huskily, anxious to be on her own to watch.

"It's wonderful how our species on so many worlds can communicate on this level," Anor cooed in the background, out of sight of the camera, just loud enough for the audience to hear.

"It's one of the mysteries of the universe." Jado explained to the masses, repeating what everyone knew, yet required repeating for a younger generation. This was similar to the admonishment that everyone keep their hands away from their faces to reduce infection from viruses.

Jado continued, "We do know that those from Cartoom and Valencia and so many other tripeds around the galaxy have been compatible ever since they discovered each other back in the old days," assisting the viewing audience in understanding how the Valencian queen of threes was going to make several babies with this off-worlder threes from Cartoom. "We all originated from some ancient race so long ago that we have no record of them. Now we're all one big wonderful family, although I hate to say it, but if the queen's husband is watching our program, she could be in big trouble."

Anor said, "I seriously doubt the king is watching. He's at the galactic star conference 40,000 light years away on the other side of the galaxy and he has better things to do than to watch our program, doesn't he?"

Lady Tania Goldura was anything but stupid. Perhaps a little flighty at times, but not stupid. At an early age she earned the highest degree in mechanical engineering with minors in nuclear physics and acting. Coming from money, she attended the best schools Valencia had to offer, yet had never been to another world beyond 100 light years from home, a pittance with only 10,000 planets in that volume of space and only two of them habitable.

This was unlike many of her more adventurous friends who had traveled far and wide. When she heard that King Goldura was looking for a mate to whom he could bequeath his fortune upon his demise—inbreeding over the centuries having rendered him infertile—she soon realized that her future lay in the acting portion of her talents rather than counting neutrinos exiting black holes. She learned everything she could about her Valencia's king and got assigned a slot number for the interview. The king was greatly impressed by her education and the fact that she was a local girl and not some flagrant off-worlder after his money. The king accepted her to be his bride.

It was a happy marriage in that he was gone most of the time while she ran the business of ruling the planet, prized for the manufacturing of scientific products and quality spaceships. With her at the helm, the planet flourished, yet she remained basically planet-bound.

FADE OUT

FADE IN: INTERPLANETARY GALAC-TIC CONFERENCE

"GNA saucer at IGC responding to inquiry from GNA saucer tracking the Goldura flag ship confirming that King Goldura has not arrived at the conference. He called ahead to report ship trouble. He should arrive shortly, pending re-pairs.

FADE OUT

FADE IN TO THE KING'S ROYAL SPACE-SHIP

Unseen, another GNA news-ship had been tracking the royal vessel once it came out of subspace into normal space awaiting the king's arrival. The breakdown afforded them with the opportunity to hide behind a large local fly-by asteroid. Amplification of the image shows a dozen or so space yachts parked around the roy-al ship, still several thousand light years from the conference center.

FADE OUT

FADE IN: ENHANCED IMAGES OF IN-

TERIOR OF THE ROYAL VESSEL WHERE KING GOLDURA IS DRINKING, SMOKING, GETTING MASSAGED, AND ENGAGING IN SEXUAL ACTIVITY

Close up depicts various sentient beings entering and leaving the spacecraft from their yachts. "Can you identify any of those yachts?" asked Anor.

"Yes," responded the crew chief of the vessel tracking the king. "Their signature names and numbers indicate"—here he paused, as if he were referring to a listing—and then gave the names of various well known female species of various planets far and wide, a few of whom were married, were media stars, princesses, queens, and renowned bohemians.

Those names were repeated by Jado, who then said, "Looks like the king has things well in hand," mused Jado on air.

"'Well in gland' is more like it," threw in Anor, or the galactic equivalent word, a statement totally permissible to simulcast throughout the galaxy, where broadcasting and communications were virtually instantaneous, once it got past the eight second delay at GNA Central. Anor knew he'd get a chuckle from the viewers and kudos from network for making that cute quip.

When he saw the appearance of the ships, Jado knew he had to work fast against Tantor, the Taunter his old business partner. He instantly ordered a full alert to arm all weapons, including the fusion laser and the atomics, then pulled the saucer into plain sight.

Unquestionably, Tantor hated both him and the GNA. Tantor didn't know that Jado presently commanded the heavily armed GNA ship and that GNA had granted Jado absolute authority to protect the vessel from foreign intervention. Furthermore, the watching masses had no idea that the massive GNA saucer possessed serious armament. They would soon find out.

The pirates drew closer and the image of Tantor appeared, in all his pale glory. A ghostly pale white-skinned bipedal humanoid from the far reaches of the galaxy, he had ruled the skyways for a generation, plundering ships and worlds alike—the most feared pirate in the galaxy, one with whom Jado had partnered for many years. "Ahoy, there GNA captain, do you have the guts to show your face?"

Jado laughed and lit up Tantor's screen with his own image, cognizant that none of the ships in front of him had even activated their weapon's systems in their overinflated sense of security. Seeing the surprise on Tantor's face, Jado said, "Hello, Tantor, I see you brought along your mother and grandmother and their little piglets to do your fighting for you."

"Jado. You're still alive, are you?" The pirate bristled with rage. Nobody spoke to him that way.

"Alive and well," Jado smirked. "While we are discussing your mother, the word around the galaxy is that she never did recognize you as a living entity, just another bit of afterbirth."

Tantor's thin, but toughened skin, became inflamed and his entire pale, almost see-through body turned bright ruby red. The viewing audience thoughout the galaxy moved closer to their 3-D screens, perhaps inhaling a nerve-activating accelerant in the process while appauled at the sight of a semi-translucent being in red mode.

"Yes, Tantor, you fool. I am alive and I told you once what would happen if I ever saw you again. By the way, say hello and goodbye to several billion viewers."

"Viewers? Goodbye?"

"Yes, Tantor. You are on the news. The entire galaxy is now watching you say goodbye to all of those who wish you the worst in the next life."

Jado pressed the firing stud on the laser fusion weapon pointing down the throat of Tantor's ship. A moment of brief shock passed over the pirate's face while his ill-begotten ship and those accompanying him melted into lumps of metal. Two other blasts from the atomics soundlessly turned the metal into free atoms with only a single ship escaping, the one belonging to Warfoot, Tantor's second in command, another semi-translucent or Semi-T being.

He had pent up anger because of galaxy-wide

prejudice against humanoid biped Semi-Ts. One could see into them, but not completely through them.

"I always wanted to do that," mumbled Jado, now a bigger hero than ever in the eyes of the audience.

At that moment, completely unaware of the happenings at Valencia, or the presence of the watching GNA vessel, King Kredo Quinn's ship appeared out of subspace and casually cruised downward for a landing at the castle of the queen, while her own husband, Goldura the Fourtieth, partied endlessly near the other end of the galaxy.

FADE OUT: EXTENDED COMMERCIAL BREAK FROM DRUGS FOR ALL OCCA-SIONS, SIN WITHOUT GUILT, LIFE AFTER DEATH, AND LUCIOUS LACIVIOUSNESS

FADE IN: QUEEN'S CHAMBER

The queen permitted the green three-eyed, three-tentacled, three legged male from Cartoom to disrobe her; all details captured by the hidden camera. (GNA never revealed how they had obtained interior shots of their subjects, nor the methods which were used to place their cameras in orbit, or when they had been put in place.) Somehow, the public accepted their presence in light of the greater truth—the drama itself. Like a good novel, sometimes it is necessary to suspend disbelief for the good of the story.

Now Kredo's sensory tentacle touched the

special area of Goldura of the Tresses while the camera panned in slowly. Beyond a few moans of the aroused camera crew, and perhaps Jado, not a word was spoken.

The handmaid watched in rapture from her spyhole, as Kredo's sensory tentacle exuded the impregnating fluid and Lady Goldura swooned in his arms as she felt the babies being conceived. Yes, the three children would come out to look like him, or so she hoped, this time a female version with three breasts to complement the first children they had conceived together. In six weeks she would be ready to conceive again, but there was no reason why they couldn't practice until then. They spoke of their next meeting quietly, as if fearful of being overheard.

FADE OUT: END OF SEASON'S BROAD-CASTS

NEXT SEASON HIGHLIGHTS

FADE IN

Warfoot turns to his younger brother, Junior, seated at the console next to him. Their mother had given birth to quadruplets in her single litter with Junior the youngest and Warfoot the oldest my mere seconds.

"Tantor caused his own death," Warfoot began.

"Sure," replied the younger brother. "He couldn't stand being taunted, instead of being the taunter. I will allow that he was magnificently bold."

"Yes, but set in his ways," Warfoot asserted. "Tantor relied solely on his spies to keep him informed of events within the galaxy where a being might make a dishonest living. He was all about business, but don't believe everything you hear, news reports can be biased. He did have his immoral code of ethics."

Junior agreed. "I maintain that we still need to tune in to the GNA broadcasts that feature these bothersome episodes. We need to see what that damnable Jado Quinn had to say about the death of Tantor, if anything, and if they have a clue as to where you and I might have gone."

Warfoot pouted his humanoid mouth. "How had that damnable Quinn arranged to arm the news vessel? Okay, he has a real job. But he was a lot better as a pirate when he worked with us. Too bad he had to develop an honest streak. I wonder if GNA knows about Quinn's background. Maybe we can get a message to them and give our friend a little embarrassment, such as getting ousted from his position and public scorn throughout the galaxy."

"Older brother, I wouldn't make Quinn too much of a project. We have other foods on the table. Besides, Jado is fairly easy to read. It's his brother, Anor, who I don't trust. The guy is too quiet, and like Kredo, he loves to party when they give him time off from that flying garbage can—all right, a garbage can with a few weapons.

"Anyway, I'm glad we didn't capture Kredo, because King Goldura is worth infinitely more than another Quinn brother. The fact that he is stalled for whatever reason is our opportunity. All we have to do is to pinpoint Goldura's flagship and capture it along with a few other wealthy hostages and we'll never have to work another day."

"As far as that goes, we don't have to work, now, Junior."

"That's beside the point. Isn't the dream to own as much as we can, to think boldly?"

"I hear you, brother," Warfoot nodded his huge head. "I'll tell you something else. I think Jado let us go on purpose. Why? Because they're in the entertainment business and we lend excitement to their lives and to the lives of their viewers."

"Which begs the question, are we being watched now?" threw in Junior.

Warfoot shrugged as if to say, "So what?" He made a few calls and within minutes, received the footage he had been seeking; an approximation of the king's location as broadcast by the Quinn's themselves.

FADE OUT: COMMERCIALS BY PUPU'S PLEASURE PLANET FOR THE PLUSH AND FLUSH; HOUSE-SIZE SAFES: WE PROTECT YOUR POSSESSIONS; UNIVERSAL HAIR AND TENDRAL PRODUCTS

FADE IN

Split screen shows a sweating and panting handmaid peeking through her spyhole as King Kredo inseminates the Queen who lathers herself in his now expressed and voluminous saved-up fluids.

Now laying intertwined, the two lovers offered an attraction crossing social and interplanetary barriers. Who could not identify with their coupling of the two. Who could not identify with the reproductive act in general? This feature that drew in most of the viewers to the series and GNA did not want to dilute, indeed, cheapen their series with a lack of lasciviousness. Even the sponsors were excited. They'd better be.

"What now?" whispered King Kredo, as though he might be overheard.

"You ask 'what now'? Why, we keep having babies as long as we are able."

"I'm sorry I was so rushed this time, my queen. We were both hungry for one another. Next time it will be much slower and much more sensuous, I give you my promise on that. Your king will be gone for some time, then?"

"If he returns early, I shall find a way to send him on some mission. You and I must be together. I tremble at the thought."

Doubtless, so did countless panting and sweating viewers, the hidden handmaid, and the recording crew. The queen's vital signs, as were Kredo's, were sent to the viewing audience in a scrolling subscreen—vitals spiking to unheard of heights.

These episodes were scheduled for prime time. Queen Goldura's promise of longer, slower, and better sex when she would next meet her lover would be one of the platinum moments of the soap opera to be replayed uncountable times on individual all-senses 3-D screens to slathering drug-enhanced audiences everywhere. The beautiful poetry of the scene would be immortalized simply because of her natural responses and true love, and not simply acts written into any script.

FADE OUT FOR COMMERCIAL BREAKS FADE IN

Warfoot's pirate ships now amassed only a few light years away from the site of King Goldura's party. Their ships possessed the highest technology available in the galaxy, basically stolen or purchased from militaries, corporations, traitors, and spies. This enabled the pirates to utilize their signals to penetrate even planetoids for information, without exposing themselves, similar to, but much more powerful than the devices used by governments to spy on their own citizens. Stationed in open space, the images came in crystal clear. Instruments detected no weapons on Goldura's ship, nor on any of the others, apparently feeling safe in this obscure place in an absurdly tiny dot in an infinite cosmos.

"I should think Goldura would surround himself with a war fleet wherever he went," Warfoot pondered out loud. "Something's not right. This is too good to be true."

Scanning the interior of Goldura's ship and the outer identifications of the visiting vessels enabled Warfoot and his crew to construct a plan of action with the capture of the wealthiest man in the galaxy as the prize.

Newsflash:

It is with regret that GNA will be cancelling any further reporting about Planet Earth. We know many of you enjoyed the low-level comedy that defined the ongoing series; however remote sensors at the site report wholesale destruction of virtually all life forms on the planet. This is due to an extremely high amount of radioactivity. Yes, they finally nuked themselves off the airways.

Instead, we will provide you with another short and fast-moving comedy: the galactic conference now underway.

GALACDEMIC

The com buzzed and Anon answered. "Anor here."

"Saucer No. 1 is ordered to cover the conference forthwith," came the directive.

"But sir, we have the king linked up and ready to show," Anon pleaded.

"Saucer No. 2 can cover it. We need you at the conference now. Send in your last recordings and we'll show them during breaks instead of commercials. That will heighten our viewership and we'll make up the difference by increasing our advertising costs," came the reply.

"Makes sense to me," Jado said, shrugging, as Anor signed off. He gave the orders to the crew who grumbled, while turning toward their new destination. Even at supralight speed, it would take a full month to reach the conference. To do that they'd have to go straight through the largest supergiant red star in the galaxy, just like they went through other stars. When traveling at their speed, why bother to chart a course between stars when you could make a straight line shot from one place to another. In a trillionth of a quadrillionth of a second a star had been would be passed through before the sensors could even register any heat. The exception to this was when somebody tried to penetrate a super massive black hole and never came out the other side, at least not in their universe.

Time exited the equation. The 19th[th] and 20th Century scientists on earth were wrong about time. What they didn't know was that at the rate at which the ships sped, if that's the right word, time became irrelevant. Travel time equalled Universal Galactic Time, as broadcast by beacon from Butrys, which had about the same orbital period as Earth's.

That said, a course still had to be plotted. Once braking began and brought them down to cruising speed, it was imperative the ship be in free space and not in the middle of a star.

Jado and Anor returned to their quarters. Once inside, Jado said, with tentacles waving about, "That was a stupid order."

Anor had stepped back in order to avoid getting flayed. "Tell me about it," he replied. "I mean, nobody expected the king to be there anyway, let alone present the keynote address, given his eccentricities. Everybody knows about his strange ventures. Hell, he can do what he wants, rich as he is. Gossip has it the man is immortal."

Jado contributed, "What gets me is the stupid conference is about a disease that can't be stopped, so why bother? We're being replaced. It's called evolution. If we could focus on Goldura and maybe throw Warfoot in the mix, we'd have a prime show. And why didn't they send Saucer No. 2 or 3 or 10 instead of us? My question is, who's making the decision at the top these days?"

"It's some new guy, one of the virus mutants, or hadn't you heard?"

Jado said. "Sorry, bro', I don't keep up on politics."

"You should," Anor continued. "His name is Xanthor Xanthus. The GNA Board of Directors paid the chief to retire early and stuck this guy in there. He's another stinking rotten mutant freak genius from Galactose and he's only eight years old. The place is crawling with newborns like him. At least he's a Three and a nice shade of green, like us. He ran a small radio station somewhere and the share holders needed to appease the mutants who are raising hell and sticking their noses into everything."

Jado snorted. "Humph, there's a world of difference between intelligence and making smart decisions. And be careful about using the word 'stinking' on the air. It's prejudicial. Anyway, I'm going stir crazy. Running laps around the ship and the rec facilities only go so far. I need sunshine and ground. It's going to take us a little time to get to the conference on Butrys so how about if we stop off at home on Cartoom for a couple of years of R & R? I know the crew wouldn't mind blowing off a little steam."

Anor pondered his brother's idea and suggested instead, "No, let's follow orders. We'll go there for a while, then go home. If we're lucky, Kredo may leave early and we'll have a chance to talk and see what he's been up to, or at least what he'll admit to."

The thousands attending the conference had their own worries, one of which was the viral galacdemic, a pandemic that began on Galactose and had spread outward via trade ships. Anor had a sinking feeling about how this had occurred. The scout ship crew that had been rescued were quietly returned to the home on Galactose and carried with them the virus from earth.

Another concern was the necessity of co-mingling with other tripeds that possessed various skin shades of green.

The galacdemic had become a serious problem, each world having to deal with a newlyborn population smarter, faster, and stronger than those tens of thousands of years their senior.

All the conferees wore face masks, which was a challenge because of the different snout sizes among the tripeds and relatively few bipeds who had the courage to attend. They loathed one another, but kept up appearances because a true civilization demanded they do so. One species that had evolved independently was completely ape-like without hair. Their intelligence was so high that they industrially mass-produced clothing, constructed advanced cities and communication systems, yet could still swing from trees for amusement. They were always polite, but nobody liked them for general purposes. They were nicknamed Tweeners because they were half-way between bipeds and quadrupeds.

To make matters worse, the masks were manufactured on Galactose where the disease was believed to have originated, and everybody knew their quality sucked. There was no quality control in place. They made junk, but it was economically feasible to do so, and nobody wanted to hurt their feelings by making quality masks elsewhere. Besides, what's a few billions lives lost or mutated, as long it didn't affect those in power.

After three months of broadcasting about the usual drunken orgies intersperced with an occasional presentation to keep up appearances, the crew of GNA Saucer No. 1 was bored to tears. Jado took another snort of espresso and remarked to his brother, "The footage of the king taken by Saucer No. 2 is not the same without us doing the announcements. They're already losing viewers. Maybe Xanthus should have an accident. Our guy is VP, so he'd move up, right?"

Anor crossed and uncrossed his tentacles, drumming his digits on the desk. He said, "You can't believe anything they tell you from the top. Look at what they reported about earth. What if it was only a lie to pull us from the assignment?"

Jado shuddered. "Now that's a scary thought. That's all we need, earthmen, about the oddest of all species, including the Tweeners, running around the galaxy. From what we've seen, their average person is, or was, Tantor or Warfoot's equal in terms of causing mayhem. They went from dirt poor farmers to space in only a couple of centuries. If I say so myself, their ability to innovate is nothing short of astounding. I shudder to thiink what might happen if they got ahold of our technology."

Testing the waters, Anor added, "If that's not frightening enough, imagine if there were viral mutants born there."

Jado contributed, "To my knowledge, nobody from the galaxy has set foot on the planet to transfer the virus, if it still exists, that is."

Anor thought for a moment. Needing to air his conscience, the said, "I wouldn't be too certain that never occurred, if I were you. Anyway, it's conjecture that the race is gone.

"Oh, boy," Jado uttered.

"My sentiments exactly. That's why we need to get back there. We need to find out for sure."

"And do what?"

"Satisfy our curiosity about whether or not they still exist."

Not satisfied with the answer, Jado intertwined and unwrapped his arms, and snapped a few of his digits, replying, "Change of topics. What if we make a deal with Warfoot do to the job of disappearing Xanthus?"

"Warfoot! Are you nuts?" Anor exclaimed.

Jado grinned, "Possibly. I think I know some people who might know where he's holed up at the moment, given his many hideouts. I can contact them through instantaneos subspace transmission. The deal is this: If he gets this Xanthus out of the picture, we'll let him have King Goldura. None of our saucers will be able to stop the capture because we're the only one GNA has with weapons. Then we get off this dumb conference and we get some real assignments."

"Brother, you're a genius," Anor said.

Desperate times call for desperate measures.

Twice the diameter of Earth, Butrys brags four huge continents in an ocean rich with sea life and a G3 sun. It has a gravitational pull of 1.5s, the galactic average for oxygen-rich planets. The dark side of one of Butrys' rocky moons is like a drive-in theater, without the movie or the popcorn. So many yachts park there that additional police patrols had been assigned the task of making sure nobody got too rambunctious and started shooting up the place. In another time and place it might be called lover's lane, except that conference attendees owned the yachts, not teenagers. Occasional ships would come and leave. The police were directed to give them no heed.

Most of the vessels parked kilometers apart, and when paired, were conjoined with a tube connecting the airlocks like bacteria passing DNA back and forth, which was probably not too far from the truth. Of the many ships dotting that portion of the moon, one was a shuttle with GNA painted on the side, and its mate, scanners had shown, was a heavily armed, very expensive yacht, not an unusual occurrence. You never know who you'd run into when you're out of the mainstream of activity with ship-jackings on the rise.

The other side of the moon housed the mothballed war fleet that had been there for millennia which was protected by an impenetrable force shield. Only the president of the ruling council and the head of the space force knew the key to unlocking the shield.

Jado passed through the joining tube to meet face-to-face with Warfoot, a Semi-T. The two spoke Universal Galactic and could sit comfortably facing one another with security forces pointing laser guns at Jado all the while.

Jado tried not to show his distaste for Warfoot's appearance. Who wants to see the complex network of veins, peristaltic motion, and a pumping heart in somebody? Not only that, but he was not offered a proper stimulant to mark the occasion after having taken a seat. That's just wrong.

Warfoot opened with: "First you try to kill me, now you need me for something."

"Correct."

"What do you need me for?"

"I need you to disappear Xanthus."

"Xanthus! That mutant? I hate mutants," Warfoot spat.

"Me too, but he's getting in the way of my career. If he has an accident, people might think it was accidentally on purpose—you know how people are—especially if my guy moves into the top spot. Maybe you could get a secret message to Xanthus that you want to turn yourself in. Set up a meeting. Promise him he'd get all the credit and he'll be a hero and maybe get elected to the Galactic Board of Governors, mutant that he is. In trade, you'd suggest he must ensure that your numerous heinous crimes get expunged and that you must be set free. You can come up with something creative, as long as, in the end, you throw him out an airlock or send his shuttle into a sun. Keep it simple."

Warfoot scratched behind an ear, thinking. Then he said, "Put something out there for the mutant to reach for, such is their nature. I like it. What do I get out of it?"

Ignoring the weapons pointed at him, Jado leaned forward and said, "I'll give you Goldura and leave you alone to do what you want with him. Wring him for all he's worth. See if I care and the public will be no wiser."

Warfoot thought for a moment and queried, "What's to keep your new guy from talking about me all the time to stir up the muck?"

"Nothing personal, but a lot of topics are more important than you. Goldura is one of them, the galactemic is another. But we need to do this quickly before the king leaves his play toys and decides to come to the conference, then he will be too well protected and you'll get nothing."

Always the professional reporter, Jado added, "The entire enterprise is job security for me. While that flap is ongoing, Anor and I are planning to get assigned to Betelgeuse, a variable star is about to go supernova and we need to move a couple billion people to another solar system, but nobody wants them."

"Why is that?"

"Why is it going supernova?

"No, why do you care about moving a couple billion people?"

"I don't. That's not my department. Other people make those decisions. I just cover the story, but this Xanthus is nuking our careers. Frankly, if you don't do something about him, I'll have to go to Plan B," Jado summarized.

"Which is?"

"I haven't the slightest idea," Jado returned.

"I take it Xanthus is broadcasting from Butrys?" Warfoot inquired.

"No, that's the beauty. He's relying on us to cover the conference. It's a secret, but I'll tell where he's at. I need him gone. He's making bad policy decisions and slapping himself on the back."

Warfoot pondered. "Tell you what. We'll grab Goldura first. No doubt one of your other saucers will report our snatch-and-grab, and Xanthus will wish you were there to protect him. I'll have it set up to take care of the freak immediately afterward. During my travel time, I'll make necessary arrangements. I'm thinking I may need an insurance policy. I don't need you stabbing me in the back."

Jado agreed. "Insurance. That's a great idea. I've got mine. Look up."

Puzzled, Warfoot looked up through the dome of his ship to see a massive creature 1000 meters across; GNA Saucer No. 1, armed to the teeth like a battleship, hovering only a few kilometers overhead.

Earlier, Anor had convinced Xanthus that the viewership might enjoy a romantic piece about the parking lot on the moon. Busily engaged in following their directive, the crew failed to see Anor slip into his cabin to watch the two negotiators, his finger on the firing button of a vaporizing laser, if it should come to that.

On the dark side of one of Butrys' moons, each being concluded the agreement with a toast in their own fashion. Cruising police patrol cruisers observed two ships uncoupling to fly off in different directions.

Another quickie to leave a vacant parking spot for two more ships to occupy.

In the short while that Xanthus had been head of GNA operations, the viewership had plummeted. With the galaxy-wide coverage of his disappearance, news-conscious patrons could only assume that nefarious events were to blame. Countless subscribers optically-tuned-in to the newscasts sent by Anor and Jado Quinn, the best of the best.

The brothers felt themselves to be freelance reporters, who expressed grief at the tragic disappearance of their corporate chief—so did the new CEO of GNA, who expressed his personal regret at having lost a beloved mutant at their helm. Everyone—well, some viewers—joined the growing number of mutants in mourning the loss of a creature who had so much potential; for what, nobody could be certain.

However, the vast majority were more concerned about the brazen wanton kidnapping of King Goldura by the greatest of all criminals. The chief of galactic police promised both matters would be investigated.

The two Quinn brothers were anxious to make a quick check on Planet Earth, but the outlier would have to wait. It wasn't as though they didn't trust the no good mutant scoundrel who got disappeared, they just had bad vibes about the planet. Yes, their transmissions could still emanate from the other side of the galaxy so the viewers wouldn't miss their regular broadcasts. No, they couldn't go when they wanted because Saucer No. 1 had to be visibly hopscotching from world to world investigating a lot of things.

The new CEO tasked them to interview Kredo, their brother, who busied himself consoling Goldura's grieving wife. He allowed the goodness of his conscience to guide him toward moving into the royal palace with her for a short time to assuage her grief. His thoughtful tenderness brought forth moans of pleasure from the viewers who identified with him in every way imaginable, and some ways not imaginable. His conscience also reminded him that he, too, was a king and still needed to make occasional trips back to doomed Cartoom, if only for the sake of appearances.

At last, Warfoot made a move based on historical fact. Back in the day, Goldura's ancestors had discovered the Valencian world, had laid claim to it, owned it, and had settled on it. Trace elements graced the world along with small mountains of gold and platinum. A freak of nature. As sole owner, Goldura could do whatever he wanted with the planet, but trading his life for it was off the table. Everyone knew the king wasn't too bright. Generations of inbreeding will do that. But if he were gone, his wife might not be terribly upset.

Before King Goldura's disppeararance came on screen to a galaxy full of watchers, several days advanced noticed was given to the two reporters by Warfoot, as per agreement. In this manner, hype could be maximized and their faces could be presented on split-screens interviewing talking heads on the other. In keeping with the Quinn family philosophy: *The only thing better than fame, glory, wealth, and power, is more of each.*

At long last, when Goldura did appear on screen, he looked disheveled. "Jado, I hope he wasn't tortured," Anor commented, slyly, to his brother, with an open mike.

"I wouldn't put it past that rascal Warfoot," Jado replied. "If I ever get a chance to hunt him down . . . "

"Easy, bro', we all feel as you do," Anor sympathized and announced, "Wait, the king is gathering himself. Let's hear what he has to say."

The Valencian king lived for the moment and couldn't remember too much, anyway, but it was fair to say he would remember his own words when he said, "Dear friends, I am being held captive in a secret location. These guys here want me to give up my world to them in exchange for my life. So I'll probably do it, give it to them, I mean."

Goldura looked off to the side in apparent

response to words spoken to him, his tentacles drooping in sadness, then returned to the camera adding, "Not my whole world, just the riches on it."

The screen went blank.

Anor announced, "After these words from our sponsors, we'll open up the lines to our viewers to see what they think and meanwhile, we'll see if we can get our crew to line up his queen for an interview."

Unbeknown to all parties, except for himself and his physician, the king had a terminal disease and forgot to bring his medications with him upon capture and died within days after this speech. This did not go well with Warfoot who got blamed for his death and who was out of the deal. It did not go well for the broadcasters, either, because it left a void in their schedule.

With no other crises looming, business slowed. Needing something to occupy their time, Anor and Jado took Saucer No. 1 on the long journey back to earth.

One month later, Jado privately declared, angrily, "Earth is alive and well. We got lied to."

"True. I wonder if those thoughts crossed Xanthus' mind when Warfoot and his boys took him for a ride," Anor mused.

"Tell me again what happened here," Jado requested.

Anor complied. "Within the last hundred years, humans gained electricity, nuclear power, air and space flight, computer technology, satellites, great advancements in microscopy and astronomy, never mind medicine. Well, right before you joined us, a scout ship crashed in their desert. Fortunately, we were able to rescue our people before the earthmen got to the crash site. I think we pickup up the virus at that time and brought it back to the Galactose where it began to spread.

Little did Anor realize that changes were occurring to earth's climate and physical structure were wrought by the virus, changes that within a few short years, would visit a thousand worlds.

Suitably impressed, Jado said, "You don't think they'll be able to reverse-engineer our ship, do you? I mean, they'd never be able to understand the light drives or our communication technology." He knew these saucers and they weren't kid's toys where a child would lay down and fly it around without going into space. In human terms, these interstellar scouts had an interior construction of eight feet in height with a diameter of 100 meters. They were rounded on the edges because their self-stabilizing mechanisms had to operate in a variety of atmospheres. As many as four occupants could be self-sufficient in the various compartments for lengthy periods of time.

"Never say never about these crazy people" Anor replied.

Jado suddenly beamed. "Don't you realize what this means? This story is bigger than Goldura or the conference or absolutely anything."

Anor contributed, "This affects the entire galaxy of viewers who are concerned about scattered pockets of mutants and here we have who knows how many of them in one place. They're faster, smarter and stronger than were their parents because the virus affects anything with DNA.

"In a word, it got loose and I daren't say anything to anybody about it. Who knows what it would do to vegetation?"

"Let's not get carried away," Jado cautioned.

"I'm only saying what we can expect our viewers to say, if they knew. It's best to keep our mouth-slit shut." Anor replied.

"I'm wondering if we should make contact with earth," Jado said.

"No. Let's make contact with HQ and let better minds than ours decide. Good as they are, these humans aren't going anywhere."

HUMANS RISING

The engineers, scientists, and government officials in the underground bunkers were aware of the comings and goings of GNA Saucer No. 1, and while a segment of their activity was devoted to dissecting the theories behind the drive mechanisms on the crashed ship, others had completed its reconstruction.

The latest visit by the huge craft spurred already frenetic activity into overdrive. Typically, the visitors would stay for months. This time, the visit was all too short. Something was happening and it couldn't be good. If the aliens wanted to talk, they would have made the attempt already, or so went the conjecture. Horribly repugnant family pictures were found on that ship; weird, green, almost spider-like animals with three of a lot of things.

From the perspective of researchers, the project became one of focus, similar to the Manhattan Project, calling in the best minds to put development on fast track. As far as the technology, it may be considered advanced by Anor and Jado, and certainly offered challenging concepts to engineers and cosmologists, such as the way the universe is folded, but essentially involved combining existing technologies with no innovative materials needed. Miniaturization of components became one focus of attention. Copy now and figure it out later.

One issue became that of stopping from traveling at insane speeds, going any speed, which explained the reverse thrusters located on the front of the captured vessel which tied into the folds of the universe. Another task became understanding how to program a ship to begin its deceleration based on its speed, which was based on the distance to the target, for which there appeared to be a direct correlation.

You don't just launch a bunch of saucers from a hidden location without the world taking notice. The technology would eventually be stolen or bootlegged, anyway, so the project became a worldwide venture. Earthmen from different countries had taken the alien ship on numerous test flights, first to the planets and moons of the solar system, then to the nearby stars.

A huge tri-dimensional start chart built into one wall was almost useless. A large red sphere enclosed the central core of the galaxy which could mean any number of things. Constellations were virtually infinite in number, based on one's perspective, although lines did connect stars and their systems. These were denoted by symbols which also could mean anything from travel time to distance, to no-fly zones. All this did tell investigators that these beings knew their way around a lot of the galaxy and had been flying for a very long time.

Three ships were lost in trial runs to the stars. It became important to see where you were coming from in order to return.

What took galactic engineers and inventors many hundreds of years to develop took the engineers on earth tens of years to mimic. The questions then became: How many do we build and where do we go? The big saucer on the moon headed off in one direction. There existed literally an infinite number of others with a 1000 ships being constructed.

Well, man being man, the reader can see where this is going. Reasoning that you just don't fly around space without something you can use to destroy something else, it's best to outfit your saucers with nukes, but not to use against one another, unless necessary, of course. The main goal is to get out there and give a shot at conquering *something* and protecting home turf.

Neither of these turned out to be the case, as we shall see. In part, this is because Brandon Barfield inserted himself into the equation.

Earth is located in the Orion arm of the galaxy, about two-thirds of the way out from the center, which is dominated by a super-massive black hole. Reportedly, the arm is notably poor for planets that brag oxygen and free water or lie within a habitable zone, save one, and this planet is of passing interest in terms of bringing in revenue for soap opera fans. Reports of its denizens engaged in self-destruction took it off the radar completely. The reality countering the false narrative is appreciated by crew members of GNA Saucer No. 1, the occupants of which were presently engaged in making a living elsewhere.

With the passing of King Goldura, his wife had inherited the planet and was now the richest being in the galaxy, and despite her husband's demise, King Kredo still felt passionate about his love. He already had everything any being could ever want, except perhaps respect from his people and eternal life, and good luck with both of those.

Enter Warfoot, a semi-translucent or Semi-T, who had no desire to flirt with a Three, such as the queen, was overheard to remark to Junior. "If you can't have the king, then go for the queen."

Taking this out of context to mean that he had designs on her, this disgusted the public at large. A Semi-T making a try for the richest Three who ever lived, was so denigrating, so off-putting, that following the story could be expected to bring in a sharp spike in advertising revenue, as countless viewers couldn't wait for the series to begin.

This female, who actively engaged herself in trying to produce offspring with another king—an almost undying love between them—would never go for a despot such as Warfoot, would she?

The queen's basic duties were simple: aside from overseeing that which Goldura refused to oversee—the technological achievements of her planet, she would throw lavish parties. She would also attend lavish parties, buy things she didn't need, and engage in closeted activities without getting caught. She was not given to watching subscription video and mourned the dullness of everyday existence, which did not reflect on the true values of life, whatever they were. That said, she did have a natural instinct for the development of science under her admin-istration and ensured that her graduates were well-placed in high positions elsewhere.

"Those damnable Quinn brothers sold me defective goods. They owe me," Warfoot com-plained.

"And you're hot after the queen. I get that. But how do you reconcile the two?" asked Ju-nior.

"I'm going to take her away from Kredo," Warfoot explained, then added, "Wait. Don't start with me looking different. I say, she doesn't really love him. She loved the thrill and thought he provided it. She has everything a female could want, except for one thing; true excitement in life. She's had none of it."

"You mean like killings and muggings and ship-jackings and worlds ablaze?" offered Junior.

"You got it. Well, maybe not just yet. I need to break her in, and I have just the plan," Warfoot concluded.

"If I didn't know better, I'd say you were in love," commented Junior.

"Oh, Junior, someday you will understand," sighed Warfoot. "To me, it's her naïveté, her innocence, her yearning to find the meaning of it all."

"And you'll be there to guide her all the way," grinned Junior.

"Of course. That is my purpose."

The handmaid was aghast at the million galactic credits that magically appeared in her bank account one day with the note: *There's a lot more where this came from. Contact me at the following number 1-8725-318277-6391-2281-5503-ABC. Signed, Warfoot.*

The handmaid committed the number to memory and deleted the message.

Warfoot, the most famous criminal in the entire galaxy contacting me? What could he possibly want, unless . . . she thought. Her heart hammered. Breaking out in a cold sweat she checked to make sure nobody was within earshot, and wasting not a moment, made the call.

"Hello, handmaid, how nice of you to reply so soon," Warfoot said, agreeably. He put the call on speaker so Junior could hear and dismissed a variety of trollops who were plying them both with drugs and fermented fruit.

The short conversation was followed by the handmaid walking with the queen in the garden later that day to reort, "Somebody wants to meet you."

"Everybody wants to meet me," the queen responded.

"It's Warfoot."

"Who's that?"

Prepared for this response, the handmaid went into detail about the criminal, because, unlike the queen, she was a big fan of GNA news. Then she said, "He wants to meet you because you're both rich and famous and you lack the excitement he can provide."

Now curious, the queen asked, "What kind of being is he . . . it?"

"Bipedal semi-translucent," came the response.

"Yuck." Yet even though she recoiled in disgust at the thought, something about the venture sounded attractive. She had seen pictures of the creatures and had heard tales about them, but never thought she would see one in person, if that is the right word, let alone be invited to be the guest of one so famous.

Before she could say more, the handmaid offered, "I can arrange a meeting off-planet. He doesn't want to be seen here. It might stir up too much resentment, which you don't need."

"Let me think about it," the queen replied, making a mental note to research the being much as she had done to learn about her husband prior to their first meeting.

The handmaid bowed and returned to her castle duties.

The queen's mind became awash with thoughts of what King Kredo would say or do if he found out about her secret rendezvous with Warfoot. Surely he wouldn't think she was having an affair with the . . . alien. How would she explain it? What possible business could she have with the criminal? Hey, it was her life and just because Kredo was her lover, that didn't mean he owned her. Besides, if it came down to it, she could buy and sell Kredo ten times over. She recalled what her wizened old housemaid had once told her. "Beware of love. It can be a two-headed monster."

It's time for the flower to open, she concluded.

GALACTIC SHOCKWAVES

The liaison between Warfoot and the Queen of Valencia caught the civilized galaxy by surprise. Although Anor and Jado knew about it, having seen their initial meeting, they agreed with the CEO to sit on the story until the right time.

That time occurred when the pair boldly walked into the galactic conference, still in progress on Butrys. Some attendees dropped their drinks when the couple appeared, others stood and stared, and countless others watched on screen.

"Will King Kredo feel betrayed?" asked Anor, over the video. That was easy to do in the dead silence of the main arena where the couple casually strolled over to one of many drink bars.

"I would if I were king," Jado responded. "By the way, where is he?"

"I think he's attending a meeting . . . hold on, let me check . . . yes, there he is. Can we get a better close-up?" Anor requested.

A camera shot found Kredo seated in a lecture hall with somebody whispering into his ear. Kredo stood bolt upright and accompanied the messenger out of the room to the grand ballroom where he saw the couple through the throng casually sipping beverages from glass tumblers.

"He looks indecisive," offered Anor. "Should he confront the pair and provoke a fight with either or both of them? Should he confront them and be polite in his greeting? Or should he turn and walk away? What would you do, Jado?"

"Me? I'd go bash Warfoot. Everybody knows I used to hang out with him before I became honest and joined your team, Anor. I can tell you he's up to no good. As for the queen, I don't think she knows any better. How they got together is beyond me."

Anor checked the viewership needle. It was spiking as more and more beings contacted one another to watch the unfolding events.

"I hope Kredo does the right thing," Jado added, for emphasis. "You know how hot headed our brother can be."

"True, if he loves her . . . wait . . . he's making a move," Anor said.

As though hearing their words, Kredo, King of Cartoom, glided over toward the couple, as only a three-legged being can do, as if he lived a million years ago in the jungles of Cartoom silently sneaking up on prey. The other bipeds, tripeds and Tweeners separated to allow him to pass through.

Warfoot saw him coming and stood his ground, turning slightly red in anticipation of what might follow. As is the custom of semi-translucent beings, they wore clothing typical of a biped. Although he wore slacks and footwear, his top consisted of a blue vest that was unfastened to reveal his see-through albino-like skin.

Kredo knew he needed to strike first, which he did. With surprising speed, he lashed a single tentacle across Warfoot face then punched him three times, each with a different arm and in a different location. Kredo then smiled at the queen, pivoted on his third leg and calmly walked back to the lecture he had been attending.

Warfoot took the blows without falling and began to laugh out loud behind Kredo's back. The queen appeared to be torn, an observation duly noted by the announcers as they replayed the incident numerous times in slow motion. Attendees gasped in their manner and quickly hit the juice bars.

"Look, Jado, Warfoot is looking at the queen like he's asking a silent question: 'Are you coming with me or staying'?"

"Let's see what she does," Jado remarked, drawing the audience in closer.

Anor said, "Her eyes aren't even wavering. She's calmly finishing her drink and pouring another. She finished that one. Now she's walking after Warfoot like it's another day in the sunshine. Who would have thought she had such resolution?"

The ratings needle spiked to maximum.

"I don't know about you, but I need a break. Let's let our sponsors say a few words then we'll return to this drama of a lifetime. Where will they go? What will they do? What will Kredo do?"

Kredo did nothing except to return to the seat he had occupied earlier, while the odd couple took a tram to Warfoot's space yacht. Once airborne, he circled the parking area and flew off.

"We'll return after our break," Anor announced.

GNA replayed the scene in slow motion and put it on a loop as Anor said, "Jado, you know Warfoot better than anyone. A lot of viewers want to know if you let him go on purpose when you blasted Tantor the Taunter. Why don't you tell us what really happened?"

Jado sighed in his fashion and began his tale. "We'll get to Warfoot in a moment. As you know, back in another life when I was young and foolish, I had just graduated from the space academy with honors. Apparently, I was one of the best pilots they'd ever had. So I joined the space police training school where we learned all about criminal activities. You can imagine that with 400 billion stars and ten times that number of planets and moons there are a lot of places to hide.

"Well, one day an emissary of Tantor approached me and offered me an insane amount of money to go work for him and his son, Warfoot, and their bunch, as a pilot. Well, stupid me, I did just that and got sucked into schemes like extortion, arms running and kidnapping. After some time, it didn't set well with me and I knew I'd made a mistake. I told Tantor I wanted to quit. We got into a big argument and I barely got out of there with my life, his lieutenants blasting at me all the while. I used to be pretty fast, I mean with you and me and Kredo growing up on a high gravity world and with three legs. In my hot-headed manner, the last thing I told Tantor was that the next time I saw him I would kill him. And that's what everybody saw outside of Valencia when I melted his bunch.

"As far as Warfoot, yes, I let him go. I had nothing against him. It was Tantor I was after. I should have done him in when I had the chance, but I'm not that kind of creature."

Anor said, "I know I share our viewers' sentiments in that we're proud to have you on our team and that you turned your life around to do good."

The ratings needle spiked again.

Anor said, "Now, let's go back and see how the queen got messed up with Warfoot in the first place. Crew, show clip 17."

(A text comes on the screen that reads: Precise rendezvous locations are not presented to protect the innocent)

Two huge space yachts coupled on an airless world. Queen Tania Goldura of the Tresses enters through the airlock to enter Warfoot's yacht.

Anor said, "Many of our viewers are in love with her. She came from a lot of money and came into a lot more money. What could be better than that? Unfortunately, her naïveté sticks out like a tentacle got caught in a vise when it should have been picking fruit off of trees like it did a million years ago."

Jado added, "No argument there. Let's watch and see how she got in with Warlock in the first place then we'll return to the present to see if we can find out where they went after the conference."

Warfoot sat comfortably ensconced in a cushy arm chair when the queen entered. He wore slacks, a short sleeve shirt and foot coverings. He stood and motioned for her to take a seat made for bipeds as opposed to the bifurcated split seam triple arm rest made specifically for other species.

"Welcome, queen. Does King Kredo know you're here?"

"I have my own life, Warlock."

"It's Warfoot."

"I do what I want with it." She shifted in the

chair trying to find a comfortable position.

"Not much, so far, though," Warfoot offered.

"True. What do you propose? Certainly not an affair."

"Absolutely 'no' to the nth degree. I shudder at the thought. Not that, just an offer to give you some thrills in life."

"Whatever that means. What do you get out of it?" the queen answered.

"I get to run your planet. You get all the money" Warfoot replied.

The queen laughed, after her fashion. "I already have all the money. Exactly what is your grand scheme?"

Warfoot laughed in turn. "To convert your billion or two population into the largest army the galaxy has ever known. To educate the populace on how to fight and take over worlds, to spread far and wide. To use the rich resources of your world to build thousands of fighting ships with the most advanced weapons we can find or buy or create. To rule everybody and everything. Other than that, I don't have a plan, although I do have 100 percent faith in myself to accomplish what I set out to do."

The queen's eyes bugged out in surprise. "That's a bold plan, I must say, but again, I don't need the money."

Warfoot's face and exposed arms remained without color. Warfoot returned, "Bring Kredo into the deal, if you want, if you love him so much. I don't care. Or are you afraid he might reject you if you side with me? Perhaps he has already done so."

"You'd better hurry up, with or without me," the queen shot, "because there's another world out there making lots of ships getting ready to go."

"What?" This time Warfoot's face and arms did turn red.

"Kredo told me," she announced.

"Who? What?" Warfoot demanded.

"Sorry. Privileged information," the queen returned.

"Oh, that game. Well, I've got some good intel people of my own," Warfoot said. "They tell me there was only one outlying world half-way across the galaxy and they nuked themselves out of existence." He failed to mention that prior to Jado joining him and Tantor, the two of them had created a few mushroom clouds of their own on non-compliant worlds.

Jado shut down the speaker output, double checked it was off, and whispered, "Anor, what the blazes is she talking about? There's nobody else out there to the extent she's alluding to."

Anor swung his head in a circle and said, "I have no idea how Kredo has anything to do with this. I spoke with him, yes. I did mention off-handedly about earth. He's never been there. Few of us have been. He probably watched our series on the place and obviously made up the rest, maybe to impress her, but what do I know?"

"The conference will be going on for another few years. We can ask him there," Jado said.

"Not there. We'd be mobbed if we showed our faces," Anor added. He turned the speakers back on.

Warfoot could be seen sitting quietly, contemplating the queen's words. "I don't believe it," he said. "And that doesn't change my proposal."

"So far you haven't proposed anything except for what you want. Again, what do I get out of it?" the queen asked.

"Something you've never had in your life up to this point, as far as I can tell," Warfoot replied. Before she could ask, he added, "It's called feeling alive. If you haven't been in trouble yet, you will be. That's the fun part. Will somebody find something wrong with it? Probably, but you have enough money and leverage to barter your way out of it. Or do you want to keep doing the same thing until you're old and wilted and wonder why you didn't challenge yourself?"

The queen hesitated, then said, "I'll need to think about it."

"Of course. While you're doing that, maybe you and I stir up some muck and go to the conference together? After that, you can say I forced you to do it for whatever reason, if you decide not to do the deal."

The call board lit up. Viewers had concerns,

comments, questions.

One caller voiced the sentiments of many. "The queen must feel terrible. She makes the mistake of going with this shameless criminal to the conference and now she's complicit in galaxy-wide mayhem. What was she thinking?"

Another caller voiced the opposite sentiment, also the thoughts of many. "Serves her right, getting mixed up with trash. It's called a hard lesson in life. She better get out while the getting is good."

Yet another opined, "I feel badly for King Kredo. The love of his life is gone. I so enjoyed watching them together trying to make babies."

In fact, the queen felt sick about everything that had gone wrong. Her innocent Kredo, who only sought her love, must now be disconsolate at her betrayal. *How had she been so easily poisoned by this scoundrel?* she asked herself. What did she have left when the one thing in her life that meant something was gone? Her reputation was ruined. What a mess from one impulsive mistake. The only thing worse than the lowest point in one's life is to realize that they're only on a ledge with the true chasm far below.

For the first time, the queen felt a wash of new emotions, each morphing into the next: great shame, humiliation, embarrassment, regret and rage. She didn't blame Warfoot at all, a Xyntx will always be a Xyntx. In way, though, she had found a hole to crawl into, although the hole was already occupied by the Xyntx with the name of Warfoot. He wasn't holding her captive, of that she felt certain. He would have done so already, if that were his intent.

"Take me home," the queen said.

Warfoot said, succinctly, "Can't. First we have to stop at one of my homes, then I'll take you back to Valencia. That's what's written into the ship's program. You don't just stop and start these things whenever you want unless it's written in. You know that better than I do. So relax for a couple of days till we get there. I have a full galley, so you can order what you want. It also gives us time to talk. If it makes you feel any better, I didn't know Kredo would show up like that."

"It doesn't change what happened. What is there to talk about?"

"I've changed my mind about you," said Warfoot. "You're not the right person for the job. Kredo's a better match."

Stunned, the queen could only stammer, "Huh?"

Warfoot patiently explained, "His world is a shambles. He's a lousy ruler in the first place. Now you're gone. He needs to be redirected, to give his people a single purpose, to turn their varied activities toward a single purpose which is to give them full time employment and make them all rich. Heck, he's only got, what, 500 million people divided on eight continents and they're killing themselves off like they're a third-world planet what with all the corruption and lack of policing."

"Why would he do that? He hates you," the queen said, puzzled.

"Exactly. It's called politics. You don't think I could have stopped his attack? Come on. When I saw him, I decided to let him feel superior. That would put him in a better bargaining position when the time came—or so he might think. Or maybe you'll want to go crawling back to him. Do you want to do it back at the conference, wait till you both get home, or just give him a call and say it from light years away, a nice warm personal touch."

The queen knew she was in over her head the way this being manipulated both his words and her. When you don't know what decision to make, make no decision at all. Torn, that concept never entered her mind.

LOGISTICS

Warfoot faced a logistical nightmare. First, he failed to think things through. He underestimated the intensity of love between the queen and Kredo and, acting impulsively, had cut them both deeply. At first he thought she might be too ditsy to work with. At the present time, considering the state of circumstances and in order to redirect her planet's resources, he might be able to make amends with Kredo, first by buying him a top-of-the-line yacht, and then trying to help the king convert his world into something useful—a war machine. Both Kredo and his lover oversaw two industrial-based worlds and their construction of quality spaceships, although a concerted effort to pay attention by Kredo would greatly help production. In particular, Valencia was renowned for its science and technology accomplishments. Unless something changed, such as, if Kredo said no, then he would have to give up on the whole idea.

Or would he? The more he pondered his new

thought, the more it attracted him. There might yet by another alternative. Regardless of whether or not Kredo accepted his proposal, he'd give Junior an assignment.

A messenger handed Kredo a note that read: "Sir, your kingship will soon be overthrown and you will be exiled. The corruption is too rampant. I have a plan to unite everyone and turn Cartoom into the most powerful world in the civilized galaxy. Signed, Warfoot. You can call me at the following number . . . " Here, he supplied the same number he had provided the handmaid.

Excusing himself from the audience, Kredo sauntered through the crowds over to one of many juice bars to get juiced. The crowd parted to let him pass, watching, muttering. The last time he had been there, three days before, the scene had been quite different. He needed to think.

Why should he even respond to this missive? Because his world *was* in a shambles and because he *would* be exiled. Where was the queen? Why hadn't the criminal mentioned her? That angered him, but he was powerless to do anything. It would seem that both he and Warfoot had left her to fend for herself.

What could it hurt to call? He'd think about it. He was more than finished with the conference. Once back in his palace, he could make the contact in the security of his insecure home a boring couple of weeks flying time away from Butrys. It wasn't as though his yacht traveled at the same speed as the GNA saucer. Couldn't somebody come up with a faster way to get around?—a universal complaint.

Warfoot seemed inpatient, or so thought Kredo, after they quit the call. What's Kredo supposed to do, jump at the opportunity to tag along with a wanted criminal? On the other hand, there existed a real possibility he could be out of a kingship soon enough unless he did something to change public opinion. He liked being a ruler, even though he had no talent as a leader or a politician. He might have to go back to the shoe repair business, although he wasn't much good at that either. He knew a lot of other rulers. It might be a good idea of find out what he was doing wrong and ask them. No, that would be stupid. The word would be out. Wait. Maybe he could join the GNA team and while he was at it, he might call Tania, if she would speak to him. Obviously, she'd taken up with a bad influence.

After wrestling with his emotions, Kredo expressed great dismay when Warfoot retracted his request, as he had done with the queen, and told the king he might have to wait because a better offer was presenting itself; well, not exactly an offer, but he'd try to work Kredo into the deal, if he could.

After that, Kredo sunk into depression and disappeared into his billion credit castle. This upset the populace further because you don't build a billion credit home with your own money. If you're going to siphon it, at least let people know their money was well spent and show yourself on occasion. The king had been at the conference for how long? Now he's depressed. What gives? Uprisings were in the offing.

At long last, Junior had returned with interesting news. "As per your request, I quickly reviewed all the GNA footage collected over time only to hear that earth was out of the picture. So I took time out of my busy schedule to travel all the way out there and found that your hunch was correct. The world is alive and well and so are the people. There are tremendous riches for the taking and I'm thinking the humans can build everything we need without us having to pay freight charges to ferry materials out there, or have to deal with disconsolate lovers.

"However, there are a couple of problems. They're primitive savages with thousands of languages who somehow stumbled onto space flight. In addition, from what I could glean from old news broadcasts, they've never been contacted by an alien race, so it could go either way once they do. It might be best if a biped made first contact and not some creature of threes, or fours."

"What exactly do you mean by space flight?" Warfoot inquired.

Junior replied, almost sheepishly, "That's a little more interesting. The earthlings made it to their moon once and sent probes to other planets, but now they have a saucer type modeled after one that crashed there a few years ago, which is no secret."

Warfoot shrugged, "Okay, they copied a saucer. So what?"

"They copied it into hundreds of saucers," added Junior.

Warfoot became pensive for moment and said, "Granted, they know how to copy. That was one of 50 exploring scouts we have which are never armed, or if so, it's with minor weaponry in case of a landing to keep away wild creatures. That shouldn't be a problem for us. In fact, it may help. But something doesn't add up. Why did GNA tell us the planet self-destructed when it didn't, and that was what, five years ago?

Junior asserted, "Forget that. It is what it is. They have a built-in space force that may be willing to join our cause, given the right incentive. Their resources are incredible with a billion steel box cars and shipping containers and ships and rails and . . ." His voice trailed off as he saw his brother hld up a hand.

Warfoot grinned broadly and threw out a

teaser. "What do you think, bro'? Want to make first contact?"

"If I do, which one of their thousands of languages do I have to learn in order to communicate?" Junior answered, scratching his head in quite the human gesture.

"This is Anor Quinn. We are breaking away from our view of the President of the Mid-Planetary Foundation stealing money from his children's savings accounts to bring you an important occurrence. Tania, Queen Goldura of Valencia, has just contacted Kredo. Let's listen in."

"What a pleasant surprise," Kredo slurred sarcastically, lying in bed with a host of jars and bottles of medications on his nightstand, his tentacles in disarray.

"Oh, my king, I'm so sorry I got mixed up with that Semi-T. Will you ever forgive me?" Tania implored.

"No," Kredo said, curtly.

Tania began to sob then related everything that had happened ending with his offer to turn their worlds into fighting forces.

Kredo remained silent, as did the viewing audience.

"Don't you miss me a little?" the queen asked.

"Not really," the king answered. "I'm learning to get along without you." He swallowed a few tablets and commented, "I have several friends here that never say no."

"Why don't you get along with me, instead?" she inquired. "Aren't you in the mood to make babies? I am."

"Come on, Kredo, do something," Jado prompted in the background, just loudly enough for it to be heard by the agreeing masses.

"Oh, all right," Kredo said. "It'll take me some time to get organized, though," he managed to say.

"I'll come to you, my love," the queen offered, expectantly.

"Yeah, whatever," Kredo responded, his senses dulled from the medications.

The call ended. Anor didn't have to mention that more steamy episodes should be forthcoming.

As neutralizing medications began to take hold, something Tania said had jarred his memory. It had to do with a space force, a war machine, building ships, and a collapsing empire. The thought occurred to him that he and Tania could build their own warships, but he had no idea what they'd do with them.

Warfoot's crusty old uncle, Scur, was just the biped for the job. His body gave away his age with blood vessels so prominent that they shaped the frame of his body with the outer skin nearly invisible unless it caught the light at the right angle. He was revered for his age on the cloudy rainy world of the Semi-Ts; at least revered by the criminal portion. He could speak local tongues and had settled worlds; however, he had yet to negotiate with an intelligent indigenous species that had a bent toward self-destruction. Based on Junior's report of the area where saucers first emanated, English would be language spoken and a magnificent 600 foot tall battle cruiser would be the ship of choice to make first contact.

Scur had spent a considerable amount of time calling many of the hundreds of ship boneyards before he found what he was looking for: an ancient relic ready to get parted out, but still flyable--barely, standing in a virtual forest of ships, its weapons long ago sold to the highest bidder, its anti-grav generator hanging on by a thread. He sent in a crew to ensure its relative integrity and gave it a test run, with the promise it would be returned after he installed his own weapons for temporary usage. If necessary, he planned to blow up something large.

Doubtless, the egocentric earthlings would join him in his entreaties to join him in a noble cause, such as galactic domination and make their planet the center point of it all. He took along with him a shipload of cutthroat mercenaries in case things got ugly.

Scur worked hard at learning a single language: English, because a lot of the broadcasts he watched related to places where that language was spoken and where the original saucer had crashed near Santa Rosa, New Mexico. However, with nobody to correct him and with nobody to converse with, he feared the effort might be wasted.

Once the monster ship landed, Scur waited for all the folderol of military, TV reporters and crowds to arrive, then he dressed for the occasion by covering every inch of his body, except for his mouth and eyes, to protect it from the vicious desert sun. He had no idea the heat dome brought about by the climate changes on the planet would threaten to boil his blood. He left the ship and walked to the building in front of him, which happened to be the courthouse, where he sat down. A crowd of onlookers jammed the small room.

With the assistance of sign language, the first conversation went something like this:

Scur: (having trouble with the 'th' and 'tr' letter combination) "If you tink I'm stranger to look at, wait until you see inside big ship out there."

Military General: "We're not rangers."

Scur: "While we're here, we'll not only teach you how to outfit your saucers with some sweet weapons, we'll show you how to get around out there." Scur waved his arm in a broad sweep to include the sky overhead.

Governor: "You want to fly and shoot us?"

Scur: "No, we want to show you how to work the communicators onboard. You'll have to be satisfied with speaking among yourselves because nobody out there knows your languages."

State Governor: "What the hell did he say?"

TV analysists thought Scur said: "You strange and we crashed and we're more strange . . . teach fly shoot sky."

After a considerable period of time negotiating and making arrangements, Scur presented his hosts with a final statement and an admonition: "We settle this now." (Here he pounded his fist into his hand.) "And make no funny tricks. The rest of us know where you live."

Whereupon the others thought they heard, "We slam you now where you live."

At which point, world-wide panic, already at a fever pitch, increased to the point where liquor stores were being sold out more than ever before. A man running for public office noticed this and proclaimed that if he were elected, he would launch an investigation into the problem. This calmed the masses, because, while the worst thing and the best thing that ever happened to any politician in the country was to be investigated. Similar to galactic justice, everybody yearned to be investigated as an end in itself. Jail time never happened to the worst politicians, because after they spent all their money on attorneys, they could sell their book and movie rights and retire with millions.

The first round of discussions had ended and Scur returned to his ship making its way over the blast-furnace heat dome where even lizards thought twice about doing pushups. Over the next week, with the assistance of professional linguists, Scur learned fast, sharpening his over-all language skills to the point where each party understood the other to a much greater extent.

This is when Brandon Barfield inserted him-self into the jumble of circumstances. In his mid-forties, Brandon was a thin tow-haired so-ciable man who had escaped from the mental institution in Albuquerque, New Mexico, and hitchhiked to Santa Rosa, 120 miles to the east. Curiously, this is the same community where the original *Invasion of the Body Snatchers* was filmed and not far from Santa Fe, where *Cow-boys and Aliens* was filmed.

Brandon was in his mid-forties. Following his escape, the sociable man would lapse into irrational behavior on occasion. Like many of those with autism, he possessed a certain genius about him. His inclined toward the mechanical. Almost as a fetish, he loved to take things apart and see if he could put them together again, as long as he didn't get distracted afterward, which frequently occurred.

Brandon happened to be in the neighborhood when Scur's ship silently landed nearby, looking for all the world like a giant pear, fat end down but cut off at the bottom. Only a sonic boom announced its entry through the atmosphere, no rockets blasting fire and dirt into the air, simply a whisper quiet settling of the beast onto the ground.

Brandon wiped his hands and left the kitchen of the coffee shop where he had found a job as a short order cook to watch the military appear out of nowhere in all their glory followed by news reporters and the public at large. The tiny courthouse housed a score of personnel which included the mayor, two judges and the city inspector by the name of Ernesto Gomez who had retired from the navy to return to his hometown after working the engine room of the USS Ronald Reagan and other heavy cruisers for 20 years.

Hot dog stands popped up like weeds and wealth came to Santa Rosa with the gathering crowds, with a single alien coming and going to and from the city hall. The noise was constant.

Brandon became very nervous. He made it a goal to enter the big vessel and see what curious machinery made it work.

With constant television coverage, Brandon noted the way the alien dressed. On cloudy days it hardly wore anything. You could almost see through its skin. But on sunny days, it covered itself from head to toe as it scurried back and forth.

At noon, one day, Brandon went to a thrift store and purchased clothing similar to what the alien wore. At 6:00 that evening, he changed into the garb, grabbed a wrench, screwdriver, and wire cutters, put them in his pocket, and casually walked directly across 200 meters of dirt and up to the ship. After weeks, the bored onlookers and much of the military had vacated the area with no threat eminent. According to news reports, negotiations had concluded and new technology had been given his people.

Upon Brandon's approach, a door slid open and a ramp descended, as he expected. He climbed the four steps into the vessel, whereupon the door closed.

Looking about, Brandon found himself on a steel platform with a spiral staircase nearby and what looked to be an elevator. He also noted three steel doors. He opened one of them and found himself in a lighted circular room some ten feet in depth that may have encircled the ship that may have measured 100 meters across the wide bottom portion. Within the room, he noted pinpoints of flashing lights, pipes, valves, wiring, and gauges. It could have been the engine room of an ocean liner.

Brandon closed the door and went to work, first to take apart, then to reconstruct. He cut, twisted, snipped, turned, and gouged his way around the circumference. Hours later and exhausted, but self-satisfied, Brandon walked out the door of the ship in the middle of the night, got lost in the darkness of the streets and returned in time to change clothes and open the coffee shop in the morning. He soon forgot about the project he had begun.

In his own words, Scur lied and promised to return in two years to ensure that all the saucers under manufacture had been retrofitted to his specifications. This included giving the pilots a chance to learn how to properly read the navigational star charts, work the weapons, and utilize the anti-grav mechanisms to their maximum efficiency.

With great pomp, Scur said his goodbyes to the world and made a final walk to his ship. He ordered liftoff, which did not occur. An inspection of the engine room found that sabotage had permanently grounded them. Every communication link had been severed. Food supplies would only last so long. He felt quite confident that nobody was going to let him and his crew use the newly manufactured saucers to return home or even to call home. For all practical purposes, once the humans cleared out the dead bodies over time, the ship might become a tourist attraction.

For the first time in his life, Scur felt outfoxed. A world full of highly intelligent mutants had outsmarted him. Feeling quite embarrassed, he had no other option but to go back to city hall and speak with the staff.

Approaching one administrator, with whom he had been dealing, he said, "Our command center told us not to leave yet. They want me to personally fly a saucer to ensure that it is up to our specifications. We certainly don't want any complaints or product recalls."

The administrator turned to a second one and spoke to him in Spanish, the second language of New Mexico. He said, "What the hell is the *pinche cavron* talking about? They fly just fine. I thought they were leaving."

The second one said, "I don't trust him. What's he going to do with it?"

"We could send one of our people with him," returned the first one.

"He's a freaking alien, man. Something doesn't smell right. Notice that he never invited one of us onto that big pear of his."

"Where's Gomez?"

"He's in his office."

The first man stood and, ignoring Scur, who had no idea of what was going on, walked over to Ernesto Gomez's office and came back with the chief engineer, having explained to him the situation.

Ernesto had spent too many hours with Scur and didn't like him from the start. Perhaps it was simply a clash of cultures, or it was something else. What you see is what you get and he wasn't getting much. He said in English, "Mr. Scur, I am making the request to visit your spaceship before we can let you use one of ours."

"Wait a minute," Scur said, piqued that this

man should question his authority. "Do you know who I am?"

Ernesto smiled sweetly and replied, "Absolutely, you made this abundantly clear to us from the start. What is your answer? Do you want to call home for mama's permission?"

These damnable humans had an attitude. "We've got aliens onboard you won't like to look at," Scur said.

"I don't like the one I'm talking to. I never did," Ernesto challenged. The two administrators high-fived each other at their engineer's direct approach.

Ernersto concluded, "Now is as good a time as any." Without waiting for a reply, he said something to one of the two seated men who reached into a drawer to pull out a holstered .45, handing it to the engineer.

"What's that for?" Scur inquired with great concern.

"Protecting home turf from illegal aliens coming across our border," Ernesto said, motioning for Scur to lead the way.

Short minutes later, the men were about to enter the battleship when a sonic boom cracked the air. The men looked up to see a space yacht hovering overhead, looking like a giant black humpback whale, sans tail, with a wrap-around window where the eyes should be.

"What's that? I thought you said nobody else was coming," Ernesto inquired.

"I don't know who or what that is and that's the truth," Scur replied, dumbfounded at the sight.

Which, to Ernesto, automatically meant that he lied. He wasn't so much concerned about the strange life forms aboard that spaceship as he was the behavior of the creature standing next to him. He'd read enough stories about encounters with aliens from outer space to know that none of the encounters turned out well for the humans. He thought, *We're supposed to trust these guys who want to conquer a galaxy?*

The ship hovered another instant, then shot off, quaking the ground once again.

Now inside the battleship and on the level where Brandon had done his handiwork, Scur headed toward the elevator, but Ernesto stopped him. *Do the opposite of what he wants and you should be fine,* Ernesto thought. "What's in those doors?" he asked.

Scur shrugged, "Machinery."

"Let's see it."

"Nothing to see," came the reply.

Which meant everything to see. Ignoring the alien, Ernesto opened one of the doors to the lighted room which revealed what Scur had reported—machinery. Ernesto looked up and down and said nothing but remembered everything. Somebody had sabotaged the ship. That's why he had returned and wanted to get away.

"Yep, machinery all right. What's next?" the

engineer asked, simply and stupidly.

Scur led him back to the elevator to the top floor of the ship that resembled a smaller version of a sailing ship's bridge where numerous aliens of various species sat in chairs of different shapes and sizes. Ernesto recoiled at the sight of them, while Scur pointed out the controls in terms Ernesto couldn't understand. He did understand that nothing glowed or there was any indication that a spaceship was preparing to leave a planet. He counted over 10 beings, all repulsive green things, but had the sense there could be more on other levels they hadn't visited. The tour included the galley, sleeping quarters, and exercise area. Ernesto didn't care about any of it, nor that Scur had conveniently left off any mention of the vessel's weaponry. If he could help it, none of the aliens would leave the ship, but felt secure in that the alien wouldn't turn their community into a mushroom cloud. There would be no point to it.

He told Scur that he was impressed by what he had seen and would be back shortly. Upon returning to his office, the first thing he did was to call the militia and report that the aliens refused to leave despite their promise to do so. Furthermore, the aliens had been ordered to stay, leaving out the part about the damaged machinery. To make matters worse, another alien ship showed up and Scur claimed to know nothing about it. In light of these new developments, it

might be a good idea if the ship were surrounded in the same manner it had been in the early
days of its arrival. Perhaps captives should be
taken because he had seen some very strange
creatures nobody else had seen and didn't trust
any of them. Their little community was starting
to crawl with alien space ships. Something had
to be done.

Within the hour, tanks began to roll in, jets
flew overhead, and SWAT teams suddenly appeared as though they had been in waiting. The
scene looked like the original War of the Worlds
movie from the 1950s with the exception that
the battleship lacked the energy to fire its laser
vaporizing beams, or any other weapon, for that
matter. If Scur had any hair, he would be pulling
it out.

BACK INTO THE FIRE

Saucer No. 1 dropped off the majority of its occupants on Cartoom for some well needed R & R., with Anor and Jado deposited on Kredo's doorstep, leaving a huge depression in his expansive lawn.

The three brothers wrapped nine arms around each other and found a suitable bench to seat themselves with blue skies overhead occasionally sparkled with red and yellow Xyntx that might be described as dumb flying balls of fur. Their chief reputation was to poop significantly more than they ate, an attribute that did not escape the attention of clean-up crews the world over. Nor did it escape the attention of cosmologists, who firmly believed that a truth to the universe could be gleaned from that simple act, if only they could figure it out.

"Rumor has it you're back with Tania," Jado offered.

"Yeah, we had a little rough patch there for a while when Warfoot stuck his nose into our business," contributed Kredo, wiping a large multi-colored bird dropping from his leg.

"Good ole' Warfoot," Anor said. "What's he up to this time?"

"He wanted either Tania or me to turn our worlds toward manufacturing warships to take over the galaxy."

"Oh, is that all," Jado laughed, pretending innocence.

"What did you tell him?" Anor asked.

"We both told him 'no', of course. He said it didn't matter and that he had a better idea, or something like that," Kredo replied.

Jado pondered, "What's his devious mind up to? It wouldn't have anything to do with earth, would it? Anor said you mentioned that the planet had been destroyed."

"That's just what I heard on the news. I have no knowledge of the place. I don't even know where the mythical rock is located," Kredo answered truthfully.

Anor said, "Well, it's still intact. GNA let out that little bit of fake news because the series was getting low ratings, even with us covering the latest developments."

The brothers remained silent for a few moments. After getting bombed a number of times, the three retreated to a screened-in patio. Settling in comfortably and plugging in IVs that Kredo had set up, he suggested, "I suppose I could take a little time off my job. My career as a king is falling apart anyway. My people actually get along better with me gone. Can you imagine that?"

"The thought never occurred to us," Jado said. "But what do you mean by 'taking time off'?"

"Why, go to earth with you. Let's check it out?" Kredo answered.

"A problem there, bro'," Anor said. "Our main transportation won't be back for a couple of years because we're on vacation and we're too cheap to buy our own."

Easing back into the chair and trying to find a comfortable spot for this third leg to rest, Anor said, now feeling the warmth of the plug-in products, "Why go there at all? Like our viewers say, 'who cares'?"

Kredo took a moment to spit on a finger to wipe remaining stain from his leg and asked, "What else do you have to do? Any of us, for that matter? Let's check it out. You've got my curiosity piqued."

Jado said, "Humor me, we are on vacation. But if we do this, we need to keep it quiet. No GNA, that's for sure. You and the queen have fast yachts. They're not top of the line, but they're still fast. I mean, I have plenty of contacts to borrow one for us, but it's best to keep this kind of thing in the family."

"Mine's in the shop now for its annual checkup. Let's see if we can take Tania's. But, I must warn you, she'd insist on going along," Kredo said softly, testing the waters.

Anor and Jado replied in unison, "And?"

Tania soon found herself comfortably ensconced with three males. She had done her homework after Kredo had suggested the minor adventure to her. Everybody knew of the Quinns, so she welcomed the opportunity to travel in the company of the famous broadcasters, especially to some remote place almost at the far edge of the galaxy. In return for the usage of her ship, she demanded absolute disclosure of what anybody knew about this forlorn planet, even if humanoids fouled the place like detritus.

Her yacht needed to be retrofitted with high intensity scanners, optics, and communicators necessary for the project, and perhaps with a weapon or two for general purposes. This minor affair took only a brief period, with money as no object for anyone, and soon the adventurers were on their way.

Weeks later, the yacht approached earth from the back side of the moon keeping it between them and the planet. They employed the long range com-links and video scanner to tie in with their satellites already in place. Saucers occasionally came and went to a base that had been established on the side of the moon nearest the planet.

"What now?" she inquired.

"How about a fast flyby," Kredo suggested. "What are they going to do?"

Jado said, "My intuition tells me that one area to look at is near where the original survey group crashed and we know where that is. What we'll find I have no idea, but these larvae are learning how to fly. And who put those new weapons on their saucers, weapons that are registering on our meters? There were none on the original survey ship. I smell Warfoot's hand in this."

"My turn," Tania said. She shot down to New Mexico and within a short time, found the pear-shaped battle cruiser, hovered above it, checked her gauges, then shot back out. The sonic booms broke windows and scared a populace already trying to deal with the reality of aliens from outer space. Now somebody new had come into the picture. She took them out of the solar system in a flash well below light velocity and slowed to cruising speed.

Anor exclaimed, "A freaking battleship? Are you kidding me? Now it's starting to make sense."

"Except that the ship is dead. What's that about?" Kredo asked.

"Somebody explain to me what just happened," Tania politely requested.

"Think it through, my queen," Kredo explained.

She did, nodded, and said, "Humans could

soon be on the march."

Jado said, "Maybe. I know that ship. It was old back in the days when I was with Tantor. Last I heard the hulk went to the boneyard. It used to belong to the space police in another era. But even that old thing should have latent energy in the storage cells, even when parked, but there was none as though they've been drained. It's as if nothing is connected to anything else."

"Which means?" Kredo inquired.

Jado answered, "Something went wrong. It died there. We can leave it alone. We can't land, because we don't have authorization to make first contact, never mind that somebody else did it. Besides, we can't change a policy that's been in place since forever."

"What if we told GNA or the federation that an invasion might be imminent?" Kredo offered.

Jado responded, "Might is the operative word. And by whom? And do what? Invade a planet that GNA itself said had self-destructed? We'd be in the middle of it."

"Aren't we now?" Tania said.

Jado added, "I say we get out of here. Those ships hold over a hundred armed warriors and I don't want to take a chance on dealing with any of it. In any case, Warfoot won't be there. That's not his style. He likes front and center. He doesn't like to sit in one place. That ship didn't just get there. You can see the depression in ground. The anti-gravs aren't even working and the military is moving in, not moving out."

"Let's grab one of those saucers and ask the pilot what happened," Tania suggested.

"Good idea. Which language do you want to use?" Anor asked, sarcastically. "We've been watching this place for so long we've learned to speak and read Chinese, English, Spanish, Arabic, and Russian."

Jado suggested, "Anor, lock in to our mini-spy-satellites. Do it before the planet rotates too much. Tania, pull in behind that moon on the fourth planet and zoom."

"Got it."

Live video revealed numerous humans wearing clothing that had SWAT written on the back. The humans entered the ship and didn't leave until a good hour later, carrying numerous black bags, ostensibly filled with aliens. Two humans led one humanoid into the nearest building.

"It's a damn semi-translucent," Jado exclaimed, enhancing the image. "That points another finger at Warfoot."

Before anybody could stop her, Tania made a call.

Warfoot and Junior sat comfortably ensconced in the large luxurious mansion they had constructed on one of 50 trillion planets. This mega-sized world bragged an atmosphere of oxygen and water vapor, along with oceans and abundant green life that had not yet been discovered by explorers. Nor had intelligent life come close to evolving.

"The signal went away," Junior reported.

Scur was supposed to let them know when he was leaving for home. He had been meticulous about providing them with regular reports and, suddenly, not even a beacon signal announced its presence.

Warfoot walked over to the monitor to confirm his brother's report when the call came. The only people who had his number were the hand-maid, who was long gone along with her new-found riches, Scur, Junior, and Tania, the queen. It had to be Scur. He said, "Yes, Scur. We lost your signal. What happened?"

Tania said, "Your guy, and whatever bad guys you had on that ship are either dead or captured. Can you guess who I am? First clue, I have all three Quinn brothers with me and we're watching the humans take over your ship. It will be turned into a museum piece. That won't help your recruiting process."

Warfoot closed the connection. There was nothing to gain by continuing the conversation. He had to go with Plan C. According to Scur's last report only days before, earthmen had amassed a large number of saucers all of which would soon be well-armed. The humans were mass-production-freak-mutants bent on spreading outward like an uncontrolled wildfire so massive it could create its own weather.

Enough messing around. He needed those saucers. If it wasn't for Tania's call, he'd be twiddling his thumbs waiting for Scur to call him or possibly having to send a scout to find out what happened. The time had come to call in all the troops and attack the lowly planet. Somebody had to take charge. By the time he was finished, he'd own the entiree planet along with its production facilities. What's better than hundreds of saucers? Thousands more.

One problem: There was no way he could recruit and transport that many pilots, even with his resources. Maybe the indigenous pilots could be persuaded to be on his side. From what he'd seen of the GNA shows, these humans had no loyalties, given the right price.

Once he had made that decision, he had questions. What was the queen doing with all three brothers? Two of them didn't have a registered ship between them and he'd learned that Kredo's was in the shop. After checking with the shuttle services, none reported lengthy trips to outlying regions in recent months, so they must have hitched a ride with her.

Something didn't add up. What did she know of that he didn't, aside from almost everything. What the heck was going on?

COUNTERSTRIKE

Jado said, "We've got it all recorded. We can send it in as a teaser and draw back our audience. We'll post Warfoot's picture in the corner of the screen as a person of interest."

"For teasing a nothing world into thinking they can take over the galaxy?" Tania inserted.

Anor contributed, "He may pull back. Then we're in trouble for teasing, but not showing."

Kredo said, "I know the queen doesn't keep up on things, and I don't that much either, but from the news standpoint, you might want to let it play out without telling anybody anything. Just pick it up when the action starts. You can report it as a sudden news flash. You know, break away from whatever is being covered and show the danger to everyone everywhere. Open it up for viewer's comments and helpful hints on how to run a war."

Jado pondered, "On the surface, you're right. I have an issue with that idea. If we let it play out, somebody is going to win. Either side will have a whole lot of ships organized into battle groups to terrorize the civilized galaxy."

"Which could cost us our jobs if GNA gets bombed and goes off the air," Anor concluded.

"Is the galaxy equipped to deal with an attack of that magnitude?" Tania inquired.

Jado said with certainty "We've been at peace for thousands of years. We'd have to gear up the old fleet stored on Butrys and that would take some time. Ancient history tells us that the Selurians amassed an armada of hundreds to attack a neighboring star system before we locked down their entire planet for centuries."

"What are our options?" Kredo asked. "We must be in a position to do something."

Jado ticked off items on one hand. "We might be able to stop Warfoot by broadcasting our take on events. If we do that, the earthlings wouldn't hear about it and probably wouldn't care either way even if they understood what we said. We can expect them to make their own move in time. Then we have a war. If we do nothing, Warfoot could get serious and take over. Either way, the galaxy is in trouble and, again, we lose our jobs. Anything that threatens our livelihood is off the table. Definitely not an option."

Anor said, "With our luck, by the time we get back to Cartoom, they'll tell us to turn around and come back here. No offense, queen, but this boat of yours isn't the fastest on the ocean and

it's a long drive out here, in case you hadn't noticed."

"You can always get out and walk," she suggested, with a note of seriousness.

Anor called it in to GNA who said they'd get
back with them. Before long, HQ told them and
said, "Leave it alone. It will take years to run
it through the council for a vote which will not
pass anyway. More importantly, it will make us
look bad."

The four looked at each other. Anor said,
"Notice they left out the part about us not spying on the earthlings. Nothing says we can't
watch."

"Looks like the Semi-T may be a relative of
Warfoot," Jado declared, looking at the screen.
"See the polka dots on the bandanna he's wear-
ing when off-world? That's their clan."

"No surprise there," Anor said.

The queen pondered her role, trying to figure
out how she fit into all of this, other than serv-
ing as a means of transport. A queen running a
taxi service for three personalities did not provide any meaning to her shallow life and driving
all they way out her was not the excitement she
yearned for. She felt degraded. Her sense of humility overrode her desire to learn more about
these humans. Trying to make babies with Kredo was one thing; true meaning in life was another. Claiming female problems, she excused
herself and retired to the back of the yacht to

isolate herself for a short time. She intended to call the criminal and see if he had a hand in the unfolding of events, but to do it without coaching from the others.

"Yes, of course, that's my uncle, Scur, you saw," Warfoot admitted, unabashedly. He queried, "How did you happen to see him? How do know so much?"

Tania was stuck, and within minutes of his cajoling, had told him everything that had transpired including the fact that the battleship was dead, only to hear him laugh. "Don't worry about uncle. He can take care of himself. He's the genius of the family. The rest of us are simple people. That said, I have an offer for you. I'll call you when you get back home."

The instant she quit the call she regretted having made it. Once Kredo found out she would lose him forever. She had traded true love for a flagrant whim.

Feeling disgusted with herself, she was loathe to confess her misdeed and returned to the cabin with a somber countenance.

Kredo knew her better than anyone and immediately sensed her mood. He asked, "What's the problem, my queen? You seem ill."

"It's nothing," she replied.

"Yes, it is something."

"Maybe I'll tell you later." Now she was back the other way. *What the heck, must be some bad medications,* she thought. But her soul ached and she confessed to the three males from Cartoom.

"Maybe we can make it work in our favor," Jado said, without judging her, scratching his head with his third leg, thinking.

"I say we get back to our vacation and quit chasing ghosts. There's no story here," Anor lamented.

PLANNING FOR WAR

It didn't take a genius to figure out a way to keep from rotting in an alien jail. He convinced the humans to let him draw up plans for some real stuff, like a planet-buster bomb, not the little toys he had given them before, but under one condition: Once they found out it could work, they'd have to set him free. He'd even show them how to mount the weapon on their saucers, which is what they did, testing it on one of Jupiter's smaller moons. After that, the humans had told him that earth could take care of itself and let him go. What arrogance.

Scur moaned, three months in a damnable saucer to go what, 40,000 light years? Couldn't the federation have crashed a newer, faster model for the men to copy? He was getting too old for this and he'd let his nephew know about it.

Before he went into ultralight, Scur called Warfoot and brought him up to date, giving him his approximate return date. This gave the warlord an idea. He waited a suitable period of time and began following GNA reports to see if he could find out when the Quinns had returned because they would have to be dropped off from the queen's yacht onto Cartoom. When the vacationing brothers did wave to the masses from Cartoom, he made a call to the queen.

Warfoot had discovered self-help. After untold years of bombing and looting and stealing, he had no desire to do those primitive acts anymore. He had matured into an different being, growing into a creature bent on intimidation and ruling.

"Queen Goldura, this is your old friend. Thank you for you input. I need to ask a small favor of you. And it won't be anything like I asked before. You know my intents. Perhaps you might like to fund the enterprise, seeing as how you're the richest person on the richest planet."

Tania felt dirty giving her reply, yet somehow, it sent a thrill through her in doing something so corrupt, so evil, that it went far beyond her narrow range of experiences; however, with good reason, she did not trust the scoundrel with her money. On the journey back, she had developed her own plan and didn't need Kredo or the brothers sticking their tentacles into it. She answered, "Well, yes, I will do that because these guys are using me and I'm tired of it. But keep it under the radar. I don't need the stupid reporters getting wind of it and you have to promise that

Kredo will never find out. I don't want to lose him. Tell me where and I'll send you ten million to start so you can establish your line of credit, then order what you want and send me the bills."

It all started with negotiating with the humans, which could have varied meanings. He had no penchant for languages and the only three he knew of who could speak any of those on earth were the two brothers and his uncle. Unfortunately, upon his return, the old guy informed him he was done with it all and had flown off in a snit.

When he picked up the pieces, what remained was an unstable queen who might flip sides on a moment's notice. She hadn't run the numbers like he had. Ten million would get him started, but he would easily need 100 times that amount. If she did rescind her offer, he might have to return to Plan A, which was to kidnap Kredo and hold him for as much money as he needed.

Despite his years of self-servitude, Warfoot was not a being of great wealth what with the cost of medications on the rise. This is especially true when it came to financing obscenely expensive operations. When he received the ten million, he had one of his lieutenants pay cash for a couple of refurbished large freighters to haul parts from one place to another in order to get his fleet together. He had checked on the rates charged by commercial hauling companies and was appalled. Such outrageous rip-offs never occurred during his youth. Another sign of the times.

With money left over and with the freighters in tow and definitely operational, his lieutenants found old boneyard warships and a couple of new ones on sale, putting a number of others on hold. This totaled another 100 million. They weren't battleship size, but they would do.

Sending the bills to the queen he waited patiently for them to be paid but received no response despite numerous attempts to reach her. His creditors began to put pressure on him and threatened to repossess all he owned unless payment was received forthwith.

Which they did. His sources reported that Kredo had not made any escapades to Valencia. He and Tania might be resting up from months together on her yacht. Nor did the news report her death. Maybe he should send a false message to the king that she yearned to see him, a message that said, "I need you now. Meet me in my yacht at the spaceyard. Don't tell anyone."

The three brothers sat eating dinner alone at one end of a table that could seat scores, surrounded by numerous servants who catered to their wishes. Their escapade to earth had resulted in facts of interest, but little of value. It wasn't the first developing civilization that flashed signs of greatness before self-destructing, like a fighter showing his warm-up skills to the cameras who then gets pounded in the first round.

When Kredo got the message from Tania, he quickly excused himself. He did not announce that he would be leaving the planet.

"What was that all about," Anor said.

"Probably woman troubles. That's the only thing that will get Kredo to move that fast," Jado responded.

Uncle Scur had his own ideas. Both he and his brother, Tantor, had graduated from the space academy centuries before and while Tantor chose a life of crime, Scur remained on as a cartographer. He rose to the top position and eventually decided to give it up to make some real money. That was when he joined his brother. His nephew was another story. Like a bad politician, he had a penchant for making wrong decisions.

Although Scur chided himself for getting involved with Warfoot on this debacle and was fortunate to escape with his life, he also saw it as an opportunity. Warfoot would never make a go of it. He didn't have the organizational ability. In human terminology, Scur held a hole card and it was an Ace. He needed to get back to you know where, but first he had to do make some logistical moves.

Returning to the castle from a day of relaxation, sunshine, and varied pleasures on Cartoom, Anor and Jado began to watch the regular broadcast of boring news when the capture of King Kredo was announced. This was followed by a call from the Queen of Goldura desperately seeking their assistance.

Jado said, "Tania, we advised you on your own yacht about trying to play games with Warfoot such as trying to ruin him financially. We also warned you this will pave the way to retribution. I know this being. He's dangerous in all regards. You're lucky he didn't nuke your palace."

"All right, I was headstrong. What can we do to get my Kredo back?" the queen beseeched.

"We'll call you back," Anor said, and closed the connection.

"Here's something that's been bothering me," Jado offered. "What was Warfoot's uncle doing with that damnable old battleship? Somebody's up to something."

"You think? Let me write that down," Anor replied, sarcastically.

Ignoring him, Jado placed a call to GNA headquarters requesting what they could find regarding the whereabouts of Scur. He already knew the old guy's background and was starting to put together a puzzle.

A short while later GNA returned the call. "We have no information on Scur's whereabouts, however, a year ago somebody paid a high price to get the plans for the next generation of ultralights."

"Who is somebody?" Jado asked.

"Unknown, except that it was a semi-translucent," came the reply.

Jado quit the call to look at his brother, who shook his head slowly in understanding, tendrils flopping back and forth. "We have to get off Cartoom and beg the queen to help us get back to earth. HQ won't let any saucer pick us up until vacation is over and her ship has the spy cameras and recorders we need."

"You can talk with her, Anor."

Anor moaned, "Great. I get to call Tania and tell her we don't have the means to even try and get our brother back from Warfoot's clutches, but we sure could use another ride back to earth."

"What are you going to say," Jado queried.

"How about the truth?" Anor suggested.

Jado was sorely tempted to throw in a number of quips to that offering, but bit his tongues. The queen would smell through anything less than total honesty, being a scheming and manipulative female herself. She also ruled a world, something neither of them had the inkling nor ability to do.

During the call, Tania came to an understanding in that, should she receive a communique from Warfoot in any manner, she is to totally ignore it as though she didn't exist. If that were the case, he would have no leverage. She wouldn't have to abide by his time frames or any of his demands. If their suspicions were correct and their information to GNA could be corroborated, she would have a galaxy behind her in support of getting Kredo safely returned.

Knowing that human eyes were always focused on the moon, as per usual, the yacht came in from the back side. Peaking around the edge, Anor tied their communication systems to the mini-spy satellites and focused in on Santa Rosa, New Mexico, where a saucer now sat in close proximity to the old relic. Humans were working around the engine compartment of the saucer and Scur assisted them explaining what they were doing wrong in their conversions. He held a tablet and seemed to be showing them diagrams. A portable air conditioner he had designed blew cold air on him. The humans appeared to be torn in that they sought proximity to the cold air but not to him.

Anor said, "Sounds to me like he's been here for a while."

Jado agreed, "Right. It also looks like he's trying to give them the next generation of the ultralight."

"Who knows what weapons he's given them," Jado added.

Anor grunted, "There's a scary thought. An army of saucers driven by war-minded humans that travel around with ultralight drive equipped with the latest in weaponry."

"Yep, and Scur was once the federation's chief cartographer. He knows the best routes to all the civilized worlds."

"Can we get a glimpse of the face of that tablet?" Tania suggested.

Jado said, "Let's give it a try, but they'd have to hold it right, although, to them, if they're making copies of our scout ship, the relative speed won't matter."

Anor concluded, "Relax, keep on track and do what we always do; spy,"

COUNTERBALANCE

Before another month passed, the face of the tablet became evident. Apparently the observers were behind schedule, because they heard Scur proclaim, "Damn, you're good. One minor adjustment to all the other saucers and you're ready to go."

Anor and Jado drew back at the proclamation, then leaned forward to view the face of the tablet they had recorded. Anor quickly sent it in to HQ for verification and within short moments received the bad news. "Yes, that is the schematic for the ultralight drive. Where did you get that?"

"We'll let you know soon enough," Anor said, before closing the connection.

"It's completely safe. I came here in it, didn't I?" they could hear Scur say in his broken and halting English. He repeated the words in UG to the nods of others in the group, to whom he had taught the language.

Jado pushed Anor aside and took a seat at the

controls. "What are you doing?" Anor cried.

"Putting an end to this nonsense," Jado replied. "If we can get our hands on Scur, he should know where Warfoot is hiding Kredo."

In an instant, Jado sped toward Santa Rosa, hoping his plan would work. Fortunately, the day was still young and he was able to pilot the ship to the planet before sundown. He flew at such a rate that Tania voiced her displeasure at the challenge to the heat shield on her ship when it hit the earth's atmosphere. Minutes later he dropped the yacht between the working men and the courthouse. Opening the door he yelled out, "Scur, if you want to live, get onboard now."

Scur looked confused, as did the humans. Apparently, he did want to live, so he ran to the ship. Once onboard, Anor closed the door and the ship rose as quickly as it had descended.

Once out in open space, Jado stopped the ship completely, set the stabilizers to hold it motionless, and swiveled the laser into position. He magnified the cross-hairs to hold Scur's saucer in focus in the exact center and to encompass the exact dimensions of the spacecraft, even as the planet rotated, ensuring that no creatures were in the line of fire.

A hand stayed Jado's arm as he was about to push the firing stud, which would have instantly the melted the saucer into a clump of metal. "No," Anor ordered. "You're interfering with their development."

Jado had received an order. He relaxed back into his chair, reflecting on the hypocrisy of that statement.

"You didn't see him try to do that," Anor said.

"See what?" Tania replied.

"Exactly."

Tania returned to default setting. Staring at Scur, she exclaimed, "Great. A freaking Semi-T on my ship," she proclaimed. "Where's my cleaning crew when I need them?" Quickly getting back on track and ignoring her statement, Jado turned his chair to look at the others and commented, "Scur, your nephew kidnapped Kredo. Where's his main hideout?"

"You can't get there from here. You have to go somewhere else first," Scur said. Seeing the puzzled looks on the other's faces, he added, "In case you haven't noticed, we're on the other side of the galaxy. I have to use marker stars just like you do. We have to go to someplace I know before I can find the hideout."

"That make sense," Tania remarked.

"What do I get out of it?" asked the criminal.

"She'll make you get out and walk, if you don't start talking," Anor said.

"She will, too," Jado agreed.

"Before we get to that, I want to know what the humans know," Anor said.

"Everything: how to find the distance to a star and program the Tri-D, time of travel, anti-gravs, use of heavy lasers, planet-busters. We already went to a good ten or more stars, some near, some far. Most of the worlds I took them to belong to threes so they could see for themselves. It's frightening how fast they learn. It won't take them long to finish the installation. Disgusted with seeing threes, most of them started talking about getting out of here and exploring the globular clusters.

"What are those," Tania asked.

Anor responded, "There are perhaps 200 or more clusters of stars around our galaxy that are bound by gravity. There may be thousands to many millions of stars in each. We've never explored them. I don't think we'll ever scratch the surface of our own galaxy."

"You do know the humans are mutants freaks, don't you?" Anor asked. "In fact, it started with them. They've always been conquerors. Now that they're probably united with a single mission, which may soon supplant their desire to knock off one another, they're setting their sights on space, preferably worlds with oxygen."

Scur looked surprised to learn they were mutants, thought for a moment, and said, "I'm already starting to regret this, but it's done. I don't know how far they'll get as far as communicating with the bulk of the federation members because humans are absolutely repulsed by the appearance of Threes. I can tell you from my own observations when they came aboard my old ship; that, and the comments they continue to make about spider-like abhorrent creatures, which includes you guys, a fact that I completely agree with, no offence. They'll more likely make better friends with us Semi-Ts or the Fours than with you."

"Why did you do it at all?" Tania asked, changing the subject.

Scur shrugged. "You mean like turn a planet full of people on the edge of nowhere into a war machine? Something to do. I'm getting old and I wanted to feel like I accomplished something."

"So it's all about your feelings?" Anor inquired.

"Pretty much," Scur stated flatly.

"That's terrific. Everybody should do something to make themselves feel good once in a while," Jado threw in without argument, knowing he fit into that category.

Scur came back by saying, "The good news for you is that there are no guard ships around the world we're going to, and don't ask me 'why not'. You'll see for yourselves."

"What an absolutely beautiful pristine planet," Tania remarked, circling a world hidden within the folds of star fields by the millions. "There won't be any nights here."

The five beings stared in awe, in unison with their appreciation of a world of green trees, blue waters, fields of flowers and running rivers with waterfalls that orbited far away from three suns with at least another dozen planets in the system. Whether nature had created the world by accident or on purpose, she wasn't saying, nor would she say whether this one would remain in the present condition if civilization ever took hold. That was up to that civilization to decide. So far, it did not bode well for it. Especially if a Mars Virus contaminated being even landed upon it to spread the nightmare.

"Plenty of pitted moons to protect the place too," Anor said.

Tania exclaimed, "Instead of the little pricks of star shine we see from the galaxy's edge such as near earth, we get coin-sized stars filling the sky on all sides."

Scur reported, "To his credit, Warfoot discovered it by accident while running from the space patrol years ago. No need to protect a place nobody knows exists. If Kredo's here, he'll be in a lone structure, the only one Warfoot had constructed.

Scratched his chin. "Let me get my bearings. Queen, get us up higher. Near an ocean on a western landmass look for a confluence of three rivers south of the tall peak."

An hour later Anor cried, "There," and pointed.

Tania brought the ship down.

"No ships around," Jado said. "Set her down with anti-gravs on full. I don't want there to be any depression in the ground," he directed.

Tania, set her down gently next to a flowing river at the end of a large forest only inches above the green grass so short it appeared to be freshly mown.

Anor said, "Jado, why don't you take Tania and a blaster, just in case? I'll make sure this guy stays put."

The pair walked in a short distance in an idylic temperature up a grassy knoll to the large home and entered through an unlocked door, gun in hand. Minutes later, they returned with a joyous king, boarded the vessel and Anor lifted off.

Kredo laughed, "I never thought I'd see you guys again. Won't somebody be surprised when he returns to find me gone? He'll think I wandered off into the forest. He just lost his bargaining chip."

"Did he say when he would come back to get you?" Anor asked.

"He said that once he arranged a meeting to collect a king's ransom in cash, he would collect me. But I didn't feel too confident about that statement." Looking at Tania, he said, "I'll bet he tried to call you a lot of times."

"What did you say when he said he'd return for you?" Tania asked.

"I laughed and told him that he shouldn't believe everything he saw in the news and you and I were only putting on a show of love because we're voyeurs pretending for the cameras and that you wouldn't give a fraction of a Xyntx's poop for me and that you had gone to acting school pretending to be an engineer.

"Then he stormed out. I think he's very confused at the moment."

"That guy never could do anything right, at least not where original thought entered the picture," Scur offered.

"You didn't mean that, did you?" Tania said, wrapping her arms around her king.

"Of course not, my love, though I did want to hurt him where it hurts the most, in his ego and pride."

"How *did* he kidnap you?" Tania inquired, looking up at her green seven foot tall three-limbed lover.

After you sent me a desperate message to see you, which I know now you never sent, I left my brothers for a hot and steamy visit. The message said to meet you at your yacht, which I did. Unfortunately, when I boarded, Warfoot was onboard and made me get back into my own ship and take him to this planet. Then he left me and took my ship to prey upon you for money. "

"Now I'll have to steamclean my ship twice," the queen complained, bitterly.

"Like a small creature lowering its sweet-smelling tongue so the insect can climb aboard," Jado said.

Kredo only nodded.

Scur said, "From what my contacts told me, after the creditors got finished with him, he had nothing left but his mansion and his yacht. They took the house, but couldn't take the ship, because the law says that even a lowly Semi-T has a right to have transportation to find work. He had no money left to pay his mercenaries so everyone abandoned him to acquire employment with other more successful pirate outfits."

Scur turned to the three brothers and said, "I knew your parents. They were good leaders. Cartoom was a viable planet back then. I was sorry to hear about their deaths."

Tania asked, "What did happen?"

This time Anor replied, "They were in a head-on collision with another ship. They were both going at about half the speed of light. According to the training academy, her flight instructor thought she might have been drinking."

"Gee, I hope nobody suffered," threw in Scur.

"If, so, I don't think they were in pain for very long," concluded Anor.

"Were any of them wearing regulation seatbelts?" Tania inquired, always concerned about the highly privileged.

"My guess is that they all were. I know my parents always followed the law."

"Poor dear," Tania cooed, " touching Anor's head with a sensory tentacle.

Kredo tried to ignore his lover's sudden interest in his brother, while Scur rolled his third eye and said, "Kredo, your father was a good king. You're the oldest son and you stink. Things didn't start going downhill for you until you and Tania became an item. Maybe you two need to reorganize."

Without waiting for a reply, Jado said, "Kredo, we'll arrange a little news report to announce your rescue. Let's figure out what to say and leave Scur out of it."

Tania held up a finger and said, "He could tell about his capture and how we found him."

Anor flopped his tentacles back and forth in negation. "Nobody would believe that. It's too coincidental for us to team up and find this obscure location. Plus, this place is too nice to mention to anyone. Let's keep it to ourselves. How about this: Kredo already beat him up once, what if he does it again and escapes in Warfoot's ship and leaves him behind on some desolate world that he couldn't find again if he tried."

"But he took the ship," Jado remarked.

"Small detail."

"I'm all for that," Kredo inserted. "Although, what do we say if he does show up?"

"We can deal with that if it ever happens," Anor answered.

"At this point, who even cares about him? As far as earth is concerned, my gut tells me they're a quick burnout. Let's go home," Jado said, with finality.

Anor remarked, "You know, this new world might be just what we need once we retire. You know, start a few more families and get out of this business."

The occupants of Saucer No. 1 concluded their vacation, Warfoot had fallen off the map, Scur got dropped off at a location of his choosing with a promise never to intervene in their lives again unless it made a significant impact on the news of the day, Kredo and Tania went about their lives, while citizen of Cartoom began a revolt.

False news held that humans were gone forever, news that once had been promoted by that long gone liberal media pundit and no good mutant freak, Xanthor Xanthus, God rest is soul, and in no way typical of other mutants (who all shared the same unpopular qualities).

Moving into the realm of space for mankind was like Cortez sailing to Mexico, like Bering traveling across the frozen lands of Russian to the Aleutian Islands, like James Cook opening up vast oceans and continents for man to explore, like man going to the moon.

Exploration was in their genetic codes. Many previous explorations, where he discovered new civilizations, Mankind engaged in the wholesale slaughter of indigenous peoples. If push came to shove on a galactic scale, this would not be tolerated. The intelligencia of the galactic citizens had their standards.

Initial visits to civilized worlds confirmed what Scur had explained, that the predominant life forms were tripedal peoples and animals of Threes and a few Fours, not Twos. This concept was so shocking and abhorrent to humans that untold generations would be required to make the adjustments, if the Threes were even permitted to reside on earth. It would not be a pretty picture, so what was the point of allowing it to happen. No Threes allowed.

Saucer No. 1 received a backdoor directive to find out the truth about what the humans were up to, whatever that meant, in case HQ had to cover themselves. This crew was chosen because the reporters could speak several prominent human languages, if they could find out where the saucers had migrated to. With some 20 times the number of scouts as the federation, and counting, and now armed, the humans could explore the galaxy to their heart's content, or perhaps go elsewhere.

When Anor and Jado did return to Planet Earth to ask that question, nobody would talk to them. Perhaps that was for the best.

Epilogue

Almost thirty years had passed since the last report on earth had been logged. The brothers were retired with a new family on the world that Warfoot had discovered by accident and Planet Galactose was in turmoil. An increasing number of mutants were being born and climate changes becoming worrisome. Anor and Jado, the only two who connected the dots, understood that whatever might be occurring on earth, was happening to Galactose and had already begun to spread throughout the known galaxy.

The peoples of Cartoom had were still on the verge of revolt and Kredo was hanging on to his kingdom by a thread, although he and Tania were no longer a news item.

Out of necessity to help develop their new land acquisition, the brothers had purchased a state-of-the art all-purpose yacht with farming accoutrements, weapons, and ultra-light drive. They still had to go grocery shopping and their wives and children demanded more than fish, ground squirrels, and frozen dinners for sustenance.

On another idyllic day, Jado sat on a makeshift bridge over the nearby stream, pole in hand and said, "You know, if we don't watch the news, we'll be fine. Otherwise, we get caught up in the nonsense."

"No worries, mate, we don't and won't," Anor commented, using an old term he had picked up years before while spying on events in Australia.

"You know we need to go back," Jado said, almost wistfully, as though something about the planet beckoned him. "I don't know what we'll find, but it worries me."

"I agree. It's where it all started. I have a bad feeling about this," Anor returned, sadly.

Jado said, "If we forget they're bipeds and are disgusted with us, it has nothing to do with anybody's feelings. It has to do with something that started there and is spreading. It has to be stopped now before we lose everybody and everything."

"We don't need GNA for this. We need somebody with brains and that lets us out. Any ideas?"

"No, but I'm thinking," Jado answered.

"If it started on earth, I hate to see what the place looks like now," Anor lamented.

"We'll need to take with us a few of the best minds we can find. My best guess is that Tania can help with that," Jado commented.

"She'd want to go along, you know. And if she goes, so does Kredo," Anor added, unnecessarily.

"We'll take our ship this time. It's a lot faster and we won't have to hear her complain so much," Jado laughed, as he reeled in a five-pounder for their dinner.

"Excuse me, Tania, but didn't you say the world was blue-green like our Valencia?" asked the geologist.

The biologist noted, "It almost looks red like the fourth planet, not quite, but reddish none the less."

Awestruck, Jado said nothing as he drove the large ship to the outer limits of Earth's atmosphere. Over the next several hours, they toured the world ravaged by terrible weather suggesting a planet that had returned to its roots some billions of years before during its formation, bragging climatic turmoil enough to boggle the imagination. No cities could be seen anywhere. The world they had spent years studying had been rearranged.

Ample radioactivity permeated many waterways, in part from tens of thousands of barrels of radioactive waste that had been buried – barrels that had ruptured to spill their contents.

Now they understood why only the occasional sighting of earth-like saucers had been reported during the past years. Those sightings related to a ship cruising around a world of Threes that would fly off without making contact. Galactic scout ships were also saucers, but wouldn't do that. They scouted for new uninhabited worlds and landed.

Whether humans found their own new worlds, no one could say. With their planet being ravaged, returning for food supplies must have been difficult, if not impossible, so supplying colonies on the moon and elsewhere would have not been possible.

No longer concerned with being detected, Jado dropped lower to find a few small enclaves of humans scattered about, mostly situated in areas associated with heat domes. He focused his attention on Santa Rosa, New Mexico, but saw no people, although Scur's old ship still stood in its original landing place, albeit leaning somewhat. Virtually all the buildings of the city had burned, most likely through gas explosions.

Moving westward toward the Flagstaff-Sedona area of Arizona and still inside the dome, the geologist pointed at the massive forest fire to the north and then, looking down, remarked, "There. A cluster of humans. Now what?"

Anor remarked, "All we can do is to set her down and see what happens. We're no longer working for the company, so first contact has no meaning in this context."

Along with a score of other of citizens, Jessica Galloway Austin and her husband, Carter, labored to level the ground for the construction of housing, small stores, and the creation of farmland. They had almost completely cleared a large area of debris when the dogs began barking, then darkness fell. Everyone looked up. The sky was smoky and the sun orange from another 40,000 uncontrolled fire north of Flagstaff, the wind blowing the ash 60 miles southward.

The last thing anyone expected to see was a giant black hump-back black whale blocking the alrady dim mid-day sun and drop out of the sky to silently settle in front of them. It measured some 200 meters in length, tapering toward the rear, half that in width, and some 25 meters in height. A large window wrapped around the front half-way up and movement of green objects could be seen behind it without discernable details.

In perfect English, a voice from the whale announced, "What the hell happened here?"

Whales didn't speak, but occupants of the machine did, explaining they were from the stars and were too ugly to show themselves, so everybody would have to be satisfied by communicating in this manner.

Over the next several hours Jess and Carter spoke to the whale and told it the story of Jason Randolph and the Mars Virus and explained why the world appeared red.

As darkness approached, Jessica drove back to the compound in Sedona to retrieve a published copy of Randolph's diary, which she left at the doorstep of the ship.

After nightfall, Kredo retrieved the book and both Anor and Jado leafed through the pages, instantly memorizing everything, all the while explaining to the others the contents.

During the night the biologist obtained air and plant samples in order to collect virus particles.

At dawn the geologist remarked, "Now I understand the sequence of events of what is happening on the other worlds. We can issue warnings."

The biologist exclaimed, "I see how we can grow this virus and make these wonderful impervious panels and a thousand indestructible products. I already have several ideas on how we might be able to combat this plague."

Tania felt a thrill course through her, something she had been yearning for, a reason for her existence. She proclaimed excitedly, "I know just where we can set up production facilities. My people can make the panels any size we want by the millions and ship them everywhere. We'll build everything! No, wait. Kredo, we'll set up more manufacturing facilities on Cartoom. You will become very popular in a short time."

"Yes, I'd like to help if I can," Kredo commented, with honesty, humility, and a newfound sense of worth.

In the morning, the crowd outside the ship had grown. Anor announced to them, "We have returned the diary. Thank you. We are most curious about these panels."

He spoke of those feather-weight wondrous panels made from virus protein capsids that measured 8' x 15' created by Wilbur Gottlieb. They were sound-proof, bullet-proof, radiation-proof, and water-proof and could support the weight of a truck crossing a chasm without flexing.

Carter said, "We built our homes from them. There are several you can have that we were not able to recover." He went on to explain about the collapse of UL-One, The City Beneath the Earth, and its location.

Only a moment later, the ship silently lifted and flew only a few miles to the north. Within the hour it returned. Jado announced, "This is a wonderful gift. We collected several.

"It may not be us who will come back to you, but give us a couple of years and we'll have a thousand for you of different sizes dropped off here. Now, we must go. We find that we have a lot of work to do in many regards. Before we leave, is there anything we can do for you in return?"

Jess said, laughingly, almost as a joke, "We're trying to level this area for building and farming and we need water wells."

"Please move back," came the voice.

The ship rose to several hundred feet and, like a flat spatula, swept a beam back and forth over an area some one-quarter mile on a side, the same area the humans had been working. This was followed by a different colored beam that played around the periphery of the square and down the middle to create hard-packed roadways. The ship dropped lower and an intensely focused force of air gouged furrows and stirred the soil for the planting of crops in a quadrant to a foot in depth as the strong north-south wind blew the excess dirt away, similar to what they had one on their own world. Still another ray, this one with a sharp hollow-appearing beam of light, created and fused several holes down to the water table for water pumps to be inserted.

In less than a day on Planet Earth, in the glow of an orange, surreal, larger-than-life morning sun, the great black whale, hanging suspended in the air, rocked back and forth gently a few times, as if waving goodbye, as it shot off into the sky with the sound of a loud crack and raced back to its home among the stars.

About the Author

Mark Sneller, PhD, is a former professor of microbiology and medical mycology. He lives in Tucson, Arizona, where he operates Aero Allergen Research, a company specializing in indoor air quality and the identification of mold in contaminated buildings. He is the author of several health-related books, as well as the Jeffrey Shenero series of adventure novels.